THE
AUSTEN
Christmas
MURDERS

JESSICA BULL

MICHAEL JOSEPH

PENGUIN MICHAEL JOSEPH

UK | USA | Canada | Ireland | Australia
India | New Zealand | South Africa

Penguin Michael Joseph, Penguin Random House UK,
One Embassy Gardens, 8 Viaduct Gardens, London SW11 7BW

penguin.co.uk
global.penguinrandomhouse.com

Penguin
Random House
UK

First published 2025
001

Set in 13.5/16pt Garamond MT Pro
Typeset by Falcon Oast Graphic Art Ltd
Printed in Great Britain by Clays Ltd, Elcograf S.p.A.

The authorized representative in the EEA is Penguin Random House Ireland,
Morrison Chambers, 32 Nassau Street, Dublin D02 YH68

A CIP catalogue record for this book is available from the British Library

Penguin Random House is committed to a sustainable future
for our business, our readers and our planet. This book is made from
Forest Stewardship Council® certified paper

ISBN: 978-0-241-79131-8

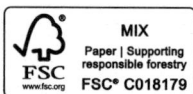

MIX
Paper | Supporting
responsible forestry
FSC
www.fsc.org   FSC® C018179

For my readers

'I wish you a merry Christmas,
but *no* compliments of the season.'
— Jane Austen, 1799

LETTER I

From Miss Jane Austen to Miss Austen

Steventon, 16 December 1798

My dearest Cassandra,

Thank you kindly for the copy of Mary's Dream or Sandy's Ghost, *which you sent from Canterbury, but it is most unfair of you to task my fingers with perfecting a new Scotch air when yours are not here to turn my pages. If your design was to preserve your ears until I master it, I shall have my revenge when you return.*

Despite the urgency of your requests, I'm afraid I cannot oblige you, or impose on our brother's generosity to the post boy, by returning the last chapters of Elinor & Marianne. *Alas, since you remained in Kent to keep Christmas in high style with Neddy and his family, while I returned to Steventon to perform the double office of nurse to our mother and housekeeper to our father, I have not been at liberty to render the composition perfect. Instead, I shall give you such an account of my beneficence these past few days as to prick your conscience until it bleeds.*

Since my last letter, I have trimmed a cap for Mary's baby, commenced work on a shift for Dame Culham and spent the money I set aside to pay our brother Charles, should he be successful in carrying out my commission, on no less than five pairs of worsted stockings for the poor. As if this wasn't charity enough, Mrs Lefroy wishes me to assist in her efforts to distribute the cowpox about the county. Be not alarmed if you return home to a village of horns and udders: she assures me it is in a noble cause.

I expect your happy party at Godmersham is inundated with invitations to festive gatherings, and Beth may even be planning to host her own. Pray tell me, has Neddy restored the ballroom to its intended purpose yet? Better still, has he restored the library? So far we have but one foray into wider society to look forward to. A card arrived this morning from Elizabeth Chute requesting our presence (yes, even mine!) at a Children's Ball at The Vyne on Christmas Eve. An odd choice of occasion for a childless household, I agree. I can only conjecture that the usually eremitic Mr Chute conceded to the scheme in hopes that the presence of so many young people might induce his wife to produce some offspring of her own. Unless she has not told him, and it will be as much of a surprise to the old man to find himself hosting as it was for us to be invited. It is a masquerade, on the theme of fairy tales and folk heroes. I already have my work cut out (in the form of my old blue petticoat and five yards of spotted muslin) and am sanguine I shall produce an acceptable costume in time.

You need not waste too much pity, therefore, on your poor relations, as we are not wholly without sources of amusement within our diminished family circle. Why, earlier this evening, our brother James summoned us to Deane Parsonage in honour of my birthday and to encourage Mary to quit her extended period of lying in. Mother refused to join us, claiming she remains too unwell to go clinking about in pattens. Since she has recovered enough strength to dig her garden and scold me most severely on my inattentiveness during my short tenure as mistress of the rectory, I suspect she is as weary of paying court to our sister-in-law as I am.

Thus, Father and I walked à deux through woodland and over muddy fields, only to spend a tedious hour yawning and shivering by Mary's bedside as James informed us of his plans to convert the cellar into a kennel, and she fretted over a faint blemish on James Edward's forehead (or Edward, as his mother calls him to distinguish him from his father. Although not, I fear from his uncle or cousin). At one month old, our latest nephew is as fat as butter. Mary, meanwhile, insists she remains too delicate to quit her chamber. After her previous mishap in childbed, I cannot begrudge her determination to recover at leisure. However, I do think it rather hard on poor little Anna to have gained a stepmother only to lose her again so soon. I don't remember Beth ever waiting that long to be churched but perhaps one grows more expedient at lying in after five children. Although I cannot see how.

Eventually, from a lack of anything more to say to each other, we resorted to charades. I know it is our tradition to wait until Christmas Eve to share our efforts, but as so many of our family are dispersed this year, we sought to get ahead of the post office by composing them early. Mine was lauded as the most amusing (by myself at any rate; James declared it 'unexcogitable' and my father refused to adjudicate). I have no doubt you will make short work of it.

> When my first is a task to a young girl of spirit,
> And my second confines her to finish the piece,
> How hard is her fate!
> But how great is her merit,
> If by taking my all she effects her release!

Mary, being too dull to compose a charade, regaled us instead with a short history of the terrible curse that lingers over the Portals. According to our sister-in-law, the Christmas before the outbreak that cut down Sir Robert and his two youngest daughters, and left Lady Isabella so horribly disfigured that she retired from society altogether, the family invited tragedy upon themselves by prevailing on their eldest child, Mary Ellen, to marry against her strongest inclinations. Mere hours after she was given away in holy matrimony to a young William Chute, the former Miss Portal fled her wedding breakfast never to be seen again. Mary insists the missing bride was immediately torn apart by wolves and that her spirit now haunts the woods between Steventon and Deane. This ghastly tale having dampened the mood somewhat, my father and I crept home by the light of the first moon, starting at every hoot of the owl and screech of the fox. Especially as our path took us directly past Ashe Park where, Mary had assured us, Lady Isabella returns each Christmas (the veil between the living and the deceased being generally acknowledged to be thinnest at this time of year) in hopes of communing with her dead relations. Father says it is nonsense and, in all probability, Mary Ellen eloped with a handsome soldier but I noted his step was sprightlier than usual and, in his haste to reach the rectory, he nearly left me behind several times in the darkness.

Yours festively,
J.A.

PS Kiss the children for me.
KCOLMEH SI REWSNA EHT SPP

Miss Austen
Edward Austen's Esqr
Godmersham Park
Faversham
Kent

Chapter One

Hampshire, England, 17 December 1798

Jane lingers at the entrance to Ashe Park, the misty morning imbuing her with a degree more courage to pause and ponder the fate of the missing bride than the eerie darkness of the previous evening would permit. Alas, all that is visible of the once grand house from the lane between Steventon and Deane is an avenue of lime, crowded with brambles and leading to an apparent wilderness. The spiteful vegetation is so overgrown, a lone horse could pass through the thicket without being cut to shreds. Between two stone pillars, one half of an ironwork gate remains upright, while the other hangs open at a precarious angle, as if daring Jane to enter. Sage-green paint peels from the ornate frame, exposing the rusted metal beneath. At the tip, an expansive cobweb is draped artfully over a decorative scroll. The delicate thread is encased in a brittle film of ice, giving the impression that a slovenly young lady has abandoned her crochet to the elements. Jane shivers as she imagines Mary Ellen passing through these gates for the last time, in hopes of finding her liberty, while her family toasted her marriage behind her.

Jane had heard tell of the apparition that haunted the woods, of course. While they were growing up at the rectory, her elder brothers had delighted in terrifying her and Cassandra, and whichever hapless schoolboys happened to be boarding with them at the time, with tales of ghosts and murder. Especially throughout the long winter evenings, when all other sport was unavailable. Yet, somehow, Jane had not connected the unfortunate Mary Ellen with the Portals' subsequent decimation. The family's grief is one with which she is familiar, owing to the elaborate memorial to the two younger girls set in the nave of St Nicholas's church. In her youth, Jane spent many hours memorizing every curl and dimple of two fat cherubs, carved from Portland stone and set in a triangle pediment above the Austens' usual pew, as she prayed for the forbearance not to yawn or fidget while her father delivered his Sunday sermon. To young Jane, the infants seemed a playful, comforting presence, but Cassandra's lip would tremble and her eyes turn glassy whenever she fixed on the words carved below:

IN MEMORY OF CECILIA PORTAL, AGED 14 YEARS,
AND AUGUSTA PORTAL, AGED 11 YEARS
BOTH CUT OFF BY THE SMALLPOX, 24 DECEMBER 1783
'IN THEIR DEATH THEY WERE NOT DIVIDED'

Over time, Jane realized that the reason the inscription would prompt Cassandra to press her hot palm to Jane's was not only because it immortalized two sisters at a similar distance in age to themselves but also because it appeared directly after the Austen girls' own close brush with a fatal disease.

In the spring of 1783, Mrs Austen announced she had enrolled Cassandra in a small private school, recently established by a friend of the family in Oxford, as a companion to her cousin. Jane, who was seven at the time, did not receive the news well. She was already indignant at having to surrender Cassandra for weeks at a time whenever her mother's sister, Aunt Cooper, invited her to visit them in Bath. She would not willingly give up her sister for the duration of an entire term. Accordingly, Jane cried and sulked and stormed about the rectory until Mrs Austen agreed to send her too. It did not take long, only until her mother calculated that, with both girls away and their bedroom unoccupied, she could take in two schoolboys at more than double the rate she was paying for her daughters' education. Jane's enduring memory of her time away was of growing impatient as to when she and the other girls were to begin the grand affair of learning, rather than constantly being reminded to straighten their caps and clean beneath their fingernails.

That was until their schoolmistress announced she was removing her establishment to Southampton where the girls would enjoy the sea air and play on the ramparts and, less auspiciously, be packed into cheap lodgings, and exposed to all manner of deadly ailments by the returning troops. After Jane succumbed to typhus, she lay in her flea-ridden cot for what felt like weeks, her head thudding and her mouth full of bile, as Cassandra stared at her in wide-eyed helplessness. Mercifully, Mrs Austen arrived in time to throw open the windows, strip the sodden bedsheets and chide Jane back to health. As soon as all three girls were well enough to travel, Mrs Austen and Mrs Cooper whisked them away to their respective homes with no more thought to their education. But soon after they reached Steventon, a stark reminder arrived of how grave the danger had been to Jane in a letter to Mrs Austen from her brother-in-law, notifying her that, although Mrs Cooper had succeeded in restoring her daughter to health, she had succumbed to the disease herself and was to be buried the following day. It was the first terrible loss Jane can remember afflicting the family and, to this day, the only time she has seen her mother weep openly.

Now, the bitter wind whistles a haunting cry through the bare branches of hawthorn, oak and ash, encouraging Jane to continue her journey to Deane. Ordinarily, she would not call on her sister-in-law again so soon, but Mary's reluctance to quit her chamber after the birth of her baby is becoming a concern for her wider family. While Jane may sympathize with the heightened anxiety of a new mother, it will be necessary to expose

Edward to the frigid air sooner or later unless Mary intends to keep him a prisoner all his life.

Added to this, had Jane tarried at home any longer, she would have been swept into her mother's plans to murder every spider seeking sanctuary at the rectory. She cannot fathom why Mrs Austen is so hell-bent on performing her seasonal purge. With all of Jane's brothers having left home, and even Cassandra persuaded to remain in Kent, it promises to be a dull Christmas. The solitude does, however, afford her more opportunity to write. That is, whenever she can excuse herself from her mother's schemes to commemorate the birth of Our Lord by dusting behind every picture frame and sweeping beneath all of the carpets. Perhaps Mary will allow Jane to distract her from her maternal cares by reading aloud while she nurses Edward, and Jane may have a chance to review her first drafts of the final chapters of *Elinor & Marianne*. She has tucked the pages, rather than her workbag, into her cloak just in case.

After the lane forks towards Deane, the tiny medieval church of All Saints comes into view. Fallen tombstones dot the grass surrounding it, like rotten teeth. Inside, it is so cramped that the congregation may hold hands across the aisle. The brick parsonage, with its sagging gabled roof, stands opposite, surrounded by a ramshackle collection of outbuildings in various states of disrepair. It was Jane's parents' first home in Hampshire, and her three eldest brothers, James,

Georgy and Neddy, were born there. It is not difficult to comprehend why Mr Austen transferred his growing brood to Steventon soon after acquiring the living, and allowed the dwelling at Deane to fall into disrepair before obtaining the funds to render it fit for tenants.

The first was the retired Welsh clergyman, Mr Lloyd, and his family (including a young Mary). The well-to-do prefer to worship at Ashe, or even Steventon, and James's congregation is mainly made up of farm workers. Added to that, the tithes, of one hundred pounds a year, are barely enough to support a humble bachelor, never mind a family with aspirations to gentility.

Despite James's efforts and Neddy's money, the old house remains uninviting. It is built on a chalk slope, with four living rooms downstairs, four bedrooms above, and the later addition of a rear wing containing a kitchen and a garret. This annexe is the only part that remains dry when the valley floods, as it does each year, making the servants' accommodation superior to their masters'.

As Jane draws closer, the cries of James's hunting hounds pierce the air. The animals are even more excited than usual at her approach. Perhaps they have caught the scent of the mutton pie Mrs Austen insisted Jane carry in her basket to tempt Mary out of bed. But as she reaches the front door of the parsonage, the pack does not accost her in its usual manner. Curious as to what has disturbed them, she proceeds to the rear of the building – where, despite the bitter cold, her brother stands in his shirtsleeves, bent forward at the waist and resting two hands on the mud wall as if in dire need of its support. Half a dozen harriers circle him, barking for his attention, but James ignores them. Dread grips Jane's heart. 'James! Are you ill? Has something happened to the baby? To Mary?'

He lifts his head, his brow even paler than usual. It takes a moment for his hazel eyes to focus, and in that brief period Jane is assaulted by visions of her sister-in-law gripped by putrid fever and little Edward's birdlike lungs fighting for breath. 'No, pray don't be alarmed on our behalf. All three of us are well.'

'Then what is it? You look as if you've seen a ghost.'

James swallows, hesitant to confide in her. 'I made a start on clearing the cellar . . . and I appear to have found something.'

'Found what?' Jane asks. He opens his mouth, but no sound comes out. In frustration, she turns and lifts the wooden hatch at the base of the annexe, curious as to why her brother is so perturbed. One of the dogs presses his nose to her skirts, attempting to pass her, but Jane pushes him away and orders him to wait as she peers inside. All she can make out is the circular glow of a candle and the shadow of a vaulted ceiling a few feet above a dirt floor. 'Eugh, it smells like death in there.'

'I . . . I thought it was a pile of rags, so I bundled it up in here and brought it outside.' He gestures towards

13

an apple crate precariously balanced on the wall beside him. The rest of the dogs bark furiously at it. Jane steps cautiously towards the wall, shooing them away. 'No, don't look. It's too awful.'

'But what is it – the remains of some animal?' she asks. The cellar would make a very comfortable den for a vixen and her cubs, or even a nest of rats.

James takes a handkerchief from his pocket and dabs his forehead. 'Lord have mercy . . . but I think . . . I think it may be human.'

Jane gasps. 'You found human remains buried beneath the parsonage?'

'Not buried, just lying there. As if whoever it was had lain down to sleep and never got up again.'

As the siblings contemplate the crate in horror, Mary throws open the window above, making them start. 'Austen! What are you doing standing about in your shirtsleeves? You'll catch your death.' One of the many annoying habits Mary has developed since her marriage is referring to James as 'Austen', as though he were the only one. 'Come inside this instant. And you, Jane, I need you to look at that mark on Edward's forehead again. I think it's worsened since last night.'

James throws Jane a conspiratorial glance, as if they had been caught up to no good by their mother. 'Coming, dear.'

'And put the dogs away. I've just got him to sleep,' Mary adds, before slamming the casement shut.

James moves towards the house, still in a daze, but

Jane reaches for his hand. His skin is cold and clammy. 'What about the crate? You can't leave it there. The dogs will get it.'

'She mustn't see it!' His eyes grow wide in alarm at Mary's possible reaction to the discovery. He picks up the crate of rags and thrusts it into Jane's hands, so that her basket dangles from her elbow. 'Quick. Put it somewhere safe until I can think what to do with it.'

'But where?' Jane asks, as she follows him into the parsonage through the entrance to the kitchen.

'I don't know. Just make sure Mary never finds out about it.'

Jane gazes around the room for somewhere to conceal the offending discovery. A maid ignores her as she continues to chop carrots at the scrubbed-pine table. At a loss, Jane steps inside the pantry. The door slams behind her as she searches for room on the shelves. Mary, ever the prudent housekeeper, has filled every nook and cranny with jars of chutney and preserves to feed her growing family throughout the winter months. In desperation, Jane sets the crate and her basket on the floor, directly on top of a trapdoor, and attempts to dispel her panic by taking a succession of long breaths.

How can the remains be human? James must have been confused in the candlelight. It will be a fox, surely. Gingerly, Jane lifts the first layer of grimy fabric contained in the small crate. Coarse red wool gives way to a finer scarlet. One regimental button, tarnished silver with the number '23' set beneath what could be three wilting thistles, hangs loose from a thread. As she removes this, a few strands of wispy, black hair fall away. A badger? No, the hair is too long to be fur. Below the wool, a fine layer of silk, once white, now stained yellow, cloaks a lumpen form. Jane covers her mouth and nose with the sleeve of her gown and steels herself to unwrap it . . . A face of mottled blue skin stretched tight over high cheekbones, and a mouth trapped open in a silent scream stares at her.

She springs up and rattles the handle of the door, but the latch has fallen. Too late, Jane realizes she has locked herself into the pantry with a mummified head.

Chapter Two

As it was Mrs Austen who originally tasked Jane with tempting Mary out of bed, Jane does not think it fair of her mother to express such dissatisfaction with her for doing just so. Yes, it was unfortunate Jane achieved her commission by such unpleasant means (screaming and shouting so loudly to be let out of the pantry that even Mary could not resist investigating the cause of her distress).

Neither could Jane have predicted that, on learning she had been sharing her home for some time with a deceased person or persons unknown, Mary would resolve to flee it entirely in favour of Steventon until the situation could be assessed by the magistrate. Indeed, this is one of the rare occasions on which Jane must concur with her sister-in-law: a charnel house is no place for a baby to spend his first Christmas, and it lifts her heart to hear Anna's footsteps racing up and down the rectory staircase once again. Besides, as the magistrate happens to be Mary's uncle, Richard Craven, having her and James under the same roof as herself is the surest way of satisfying Jane's curiosity as to the progress of Mr Craven's investigation.

Mary, too, seems most gratified with the arrangement, having occupied the bedroom usually reserved for Jane's former cousin, now sister-in-law, Eliza at this time of year. Even James has forgiven Jane for failing to keep the discovery of human remains under his floorboards secret from his wife, since it has had the unintended consequence of restoring him to his father's house. And, really, the additional inhabitants represent no imposition to Mrs Austen. It is Jane and Rosalee, the family's latest short-tempered, red-faced maid, who are called upon to answer their constant demands for glasses of water and warming pans.

'I must say, this old chimneypiece does very well.' Mary, in Mr Austen's usual armchair, reclines in the family parlour, her feet propped on Jane's piano stool, to nurse Edward, as the family wait to hear the outcome of Mr Craven's examination of James's grim discovery. 'It's not as elegant as the one at Deane, I grant you. But that always smokes, no matter how recently the chimney has been swept.' With Mary's constant remarks on the superiority of the rectory to the parsonage, Jane is beginning to fear she is anticipating a day when she might be mistress here. Perhaps that is why Mrs Austen has been gritting her teeth since her daughter-in-law's arrival. As Neddy was awarded the estate of Steventon by his adoptive mother, Mrs Knight, the living *will* be his to dispose of after Mr Austen's demise, and it is not unreasonable to expect he may bestow it on his brother. At least, until one of his own sons is old enough to benefit from it. At this realization, Jane has never been more anxious for her father's health.

'It will soon be time to bring in the yuletide log, Father,' she says, hoping to remind Mary that he is not dead yet.

'Oh, Jane, I'm getting too old to engage in such traditions,' replies Mr Austen, rubbing his spine for effect. With his usual seat occupied, he has joined Jane and Anna at the table, encroaching on their efforts to cut out a new dress for Anna's doll by spreading his newspaper over the cherrywood surface.

'Can't you ask one of the farm men to help?' Thankfully, the children's presence in the house caused Mrs Austen to relent on her earlier proclamation against evergreens until every inch of the rectory, inside and out, had been scrubbed clean and Jane has since ensured the parlour sings with the scent of yew, fir, and even oranges studded with cloves. But it will not truly feel like Christmas until her father has selected the most enormous log he can find to burn throughout yuletide.

'I would not trust a single one of those blackguards to wield an axe. By Jove! The lot of them have been drunk since St Nicholas's Day. Besides, there's no point as we cannot light it until your mother remembers where she placed the remainder of last year's log.'

It is customary to set the yuletide log ablaze with a piece of kindling preserved from the previous

Christmas's offering. However, judging from Mrs Austen's creased brow as she busies herself around the sideboard trying to find it, this vital object may not have survived her seasonal tidying. 'I put it somewhere safe, I'm sure . . .'

'I've no doubt you did, my dear.'

'You must ask Austen to gather the log, once he returns from his appointment with Uncle Richard. It will be no object to him.' Mary sighs. Unlike most unions Jane has observed, the two years of marriage between James and Mary have served only to increase him in her estimation. If her brother's aim was to provide himself with an adoring wife, even at the expense of all other qualities, he could not have made a better choice. 'And then we can light it on Christmas Eve with the piece I put by from last year.'

'You expect to be still with us by then?' Mrs Austen's high-pitched tone betrays her alarm at her daughter-in-law's continued presence. 'I wouldn't have thought it would take that long to clear a few bones out of the root cellar.' With Mary's widowed mother, Mrs Lloyd, having removed to a smaller, cheaper dwelling, thirty miles away in Ibthorpe since her daughter's marriage, the Austens are James and Mary's only option of alternative accommodation in proximity to his duties. Jane raises her eyebrows at Anna's doll, causing the little girl to giggle. It continually surprises her how quick her niece is to catch on to her jests, usually faster than her fully grown relations.

'Oh, but it's not just ensuring all the remains are removed. I shan't sleep easy at the parsonage until I'm satisfied the unfortunate soul has been laid to rest at an appropriate location,' frets Mary. For the sake of her mother's nerves, Jane does not point out that, unless Mr Craven can identify to whom the head belonged and what it was doing in the cellar at Deane, the authorities cannot possibly know the most appropriate place for it to be laid to rest. Regardless, the family sit as if in quiet contemplation of this morbid conundrum until the sound of horses' hoofs in the lane carries over the crackling fire.

'That must be James now.' Jane moves to the window.

Outside, James dismounts his hunter and hands the reins to one of her father's labourers, who, by his red nose and unsteady gait, does indeed look to be in his cups already. She expects James will tell them that, after examining the remains and where they were found, Mr Craven will have resolved to refer the matter to the coroner. It does not seem likely to her that someone who died in wholly unsuspicious circumstances would be left to moulder. Unless whoever it was entered the cellar of their own volition and died of natural causes.

'Wait! Edward's bonnet has come undone,' Mary calls, too late to prevent Jane from throwing open the entrance to the parlour before James has secured the front door, sending a fierce draught through the rectory.

'What did Mr Craven say?'

James blinks at her. 'Can a man not quench his thirst before facing such an interrogation?'

Jane bites down her frustration, knowing that she will not have an answer until his demand is met. Never mind that she is neither his wife nor his maid, and James knows perfectly well where the water jug is kept. After entering the kitchen in such a dash that poor Rosalee drops her mixing bowl, which smashes on the floor, Jane returns to find her brother leaning over Mary's shoulder to coo at Edward while Anna hangs off his leg. 'Well, when is the inquest to be?'

'Inquest?' James squints up at her. 'Mr Craven did not think it necessary to hold an inquest. The remains shall be entered into the common grave at Deane as soon as the ground is soft enough to dig.'

'But . . .' Jane's brow furrows. She is stupefied by the magistrate's lack of assiduousness. 'How can he decide so without establishing to whom the remains belonged? Or how they came to be there?'

'Ah . . .' James stands tall, tucking his thumb into his lapel and staring into the middle distance, as if readying himself to deliver a sermon. 'Mr Craven noted that the deceased was wearing a regimental coat and, by the condition of the remains, had been dead for some time. He therefore concluded he must have been a soldier, possibly fallen on hard times after the close of the American war and traipsing the countryside looking for charity. I explained that the parsonage had lain empty for several years, and therefore we concluded he must have crawled into the cellar for warmth and frozen to death.'

Mr and Mrs Austen nod thoughtfully, as Mary beams up at her husband.

Jane, however, is not inclined to applaud Mr Craven or James for their skills at detection. 'A soldier, returned from the American war?'

'Yes.'

While Jane doubts any soldier cunning enough to survive active service would crawl into a hole in a wall and freeze to death before pawning his buttons, she knows from experience that there is little point in contradicting James or Mr Craven. If she wishes to challenge their findings, she will need evidence. 'Did Mr Craven recognize the crest on the button as belonging to a regiment that had served in the colonies?'

'No, I . . . I don't think so. At least, if he did, he did not tell me.'

'And were any other items of clothing found on the corpse's person?'

'Only a few old rags.'

The white silk Jane recalls running through her fingers was certainly not a rag. She is beginning to regret not examining the contents of the crate more thoroughly when she had the chance. 'No boots?'

James scratches the curls at his right temple. 'No.'

'It's not unusual to meet beggars roaming the countryside with no shoes, Jane,' Mrs Austen interjects, on behalf of her son's pride.

'No,' agrees Jane. 'And yet it would be unusual to meet one who has surrendered his boots but retains his buttons, especially in weather cold enough to freeze to death.'

James frowns, his confidence wavering. 'I suppose they might have rotted away. It was only the head that was mummified. The rest . . . well, it was more of a skeleton.'

The family gasp in horror, as Jane considers this discrepancy. 'And you're certain you emptied the cellar fully?'

'Yes, I . . . That is, Jack Smith was very thorough.'

'You made Jack do it?' Mrs Austen's eyebrows shoot up in alarm. 'Good Lord! I hope Georgy wasn't with him.' Jack Smith is Jane's brother Georgy's companion. Since he was a boy he has been employed by Mr Austen to ensure Georgy, who is mute and struggles somewhat with his comprehension, comes to no harm.

'Jack volunteered! And, no, of course Georgy was not with him at the time,' James clarifies. 'Jack said his mother would not forgive him if he failed to ensure the remains were retrieved with dignity.'

This Jane can well believe. Jack's mother, Dame Culham, was previously the Austen children's nurse, and is an experienced midwife. As such, she is often called to lay out the dead and will have instilled the same respect for the rituals of death in her son. 'He swept every corner of the cellar but, apart from the one skeleton and what you saw in that apple crate, there were only a few broken clay pipes and bits of smashed crockery.'

'You keep saying *he*. Did you and Mr Craven lay out the bones, to see if the skeleton amounted to the size of a man?'

'Goodness, no.' James shudders. 'But I must admit that, once all the bones were gathered together and placed into a box, he did appear to be rather slight . . .'

'And although the long dark hair on the scalp was well preserved, I don't recall any whiskers. Do you?'

'Jane, must you?' Mrs Austen is thoroughly disgusted by her daughter's observations. 'And in front of the children . . .'

Thankfully, as well as being far too young to understand, Edward has fallen asleep, drunk on his mother's milk, and Anna's attention has turned to lining up the pine cones Jane has gathered as Christmas ornaments along the table.

James runs the flat of his hand over his own smooth chin. 'He might have shaved them off?'

'Hmm . . .' Jane ponders. Granted, she has not made the acquaintance of many vagrants, but none of those she has met, usually begging at the door of the rectory or gathered around the poorhouse in Basingstoke, have been clean-shaven. 'Perhaps, rather than make conjectures as to why one of the King's men would be so slight, devoid of facial hair, and retain his buttons while selling his boots and freezing to death in a disused cellar, we should consider some simpler explanation.'

'Such as?' asks James.

'Perhaps the remains are not those of a soldier, or of a man, at all. They could, for example, belong to a woman . . . A woman who is known to have gone missing from this very neighbourhood some time ago. Remind me again of when the eldest Portal girl disappeared.' Jane says, to no one in particular, given she knows very well that the young lady has not been seen since December 1782.

Mr Austen, being the first, as usual, to catch his daughter's meaning, contorts his usually placid features into a stern frown. 'Jane, no.'

'What?' She raises her brow, feigning innocence at her father's knowing tone. The most reasonable explanation as to whom the remains belonged is so obvious that it hardly needs a genius to decipher.

'Mary Ellen Portal!' Mary shrieks, proving Jane's point. 'That would explain why she haunts the woods.'

Mr Austen groans. 'Now look what you've unleashed.'

'Me? I didn't murder the poor girl and place her in the cellar, Pappa,' says Jane. 'But, pray, let us consider this rationally. Mother, you described it as a "root cellar". Does that mean you used it as a storehouse during your time in Deane?'

'Yes, it was the best place to preserve an abundance of the harvest.'

Jane nods. 'So it follows that the corpse must have appeared in the cellar some time after our family vacated the parsonage. When was that?'

'Let me think. I was still nursing Neddy when we arrived here. So, 1768?'

'And, Mary, can you recall if the cellar was in use during your time at the parsonage?'

'Oh, no, my mother did not need to grow her own vegetables. Not when Father was alive,' she replies, to the consternation of Mrs Austen, whose vegetable garden is second only to her poultry yard in her list of accomplishments. 'But I'm sure I would have noticed if a vagrant had broken into the parsonage and taken up residence in the cellar.'

Jane nods. Mary may be lacking in many attributes, but her ear for scandal is faultless. 'And when did your father take possession?'

'It was February 1783, almost a year to the day after we lost dear little Charles.' Mary clutches Edward tighter as she remembers her late brother. 'Martha and I were still very frail, and Father hoped the air in Hampshire might help us to recover our strength, as well as our spirits. And to think, all that time Mamma tended Lady Isabella through her illness, her daughter's remains may have been under our floorboards.'

'Your mother tended her?' asks Jane. While recounting the downfall of the House of Portal, Mary had been keen to give the impression she was tight with the family. But, given her sister-in-law's tendency to inflate the importance of her own role in describing any mildly interesting event, Jane had assumed this was mere exaggeration.

'Who else would have been willing to?' Mary lowers her gaze, reflexively tucking her pitted cheeks into the frilled collar of her wrapper. The fortunate few, if they can be called so, who survive an outbreak of the smallpox are said to be granted immunity to all future instances of the disease. It is a benefit for which the Lloyds paid dearly, with the loss of their only son.

'But, Jane,' says James, 'Mr Craven suggested the vagrant crawled inside through the hatch. That was why he lay in the cellar, rather than the house. Therefore he could have arrived at the parsonage after the Lloyds had occupied it. Forgive me, Mary, I know it's a distressing thought, but if he was already ailing, and died soon after, his entrance *might* have gone unnoticed by your family.'

'Yes, but . . .' Mary bites her lip, struggling to contradict her husband. 'That couldn't have been the case, as one of the first improvements my father made after we arrived was to build a woodshed, which completely covered the hatch. Don't you remember, Austen? You dismantled it when we took possession, and that was when you came up with the idea of converting the cellar into a kennel.'

'So I did.' James rubs the back of his neck, defeated by his own reasoning. 'I was worried it would collapse and bring down the annexe with it. But Mary Ellen was so excessively pretty! It is deplorable to consider that ghastly fright might have been the remains of her lovely face,' he continues, seemingly unaware of

Mary's discomfort at his fond reminiscence of another woman's beauty.

'Nevertheless, if it is her, we must not shrink from proving so.' Jane sighs, picturing the heartbreaking memorial Lady Isabella had constructed to her youngest daughters. All these years, the congregation at St Nicholas's have been called on to mourn the plight of two perfect cherubs, when there should have been three. 'I expect it would bring Lady Isabella solace to know what became of her eldest daughter. No matter how terrible the truth, nothing can be worse than not knowing.'

Mr Austen slams his hand on the table, startling all present and causing several of Anna's pine cones to roll onto the floor. 'No, no, no. We shall not have another Christmas ruined by our family becoming entangled in a death that is of no consequence to us. For God's sake, Jane, I forbid you to insert yourself into Mr Craven's investigation. Promise me you will not bother the magistrate with your suppositions.'

'Very well,' Jane replies tartly.

But, really, Mr Austen should know to be more specific in his instructions to his youngest daughter or else satisfy himself with Jane attending to the letter rather than the spirit of his command. Sincerely, she has no intention of inserting herself into Mr Craven's investigation. The magistrate, however, might want to benefit from hers.

LETTER 2

From Miss Jane Austen to Miss Austen

Steventon, 20 December 1798

My dearest Cassandra,

I take back my previous lament – we are no longer starved for company at the rectory. In fact, it might be said we have an excess. Although it is not as overpopulated here as at Deane, where James had the misfortune to discover an uninvited guest mouldering in the cellar. We cannot yet say with any certainty to whom the corpse (or, rather, skeleton) belonged, or how it came to reside with our brother and sister-in-law, but I have my suspicions owing to the parsonage standing empty at the time of Mary Ellen Portal's disappearance. What I cannot divine is whether the unfortunate soul died as a result of her own misadventure, or foul play on the part of another. Speaking of foul, rather fowl, my mother would like me to consult you on which turkey to send to Godmersham. I dare not give my opinion, but the white one frequently attacks me whenever I cross the yard.

Yours,
J.A.

PS Tease Beth on the matter of the turkey for me. I'm quite sure she would prefer game.

Miss Austen
Edward Austen's Esqr
Godmersham Park
Faversham
Kent

LETTER 3

From Edward Austen Esqr to Miss Jane Austen

Godmersham Park, 21 December 1798

Dear Jane,

Cassy charged me with writing as she has taken Fanny to the Goodnestone fair in search of gold paper. I did not go as I have a heavy cold, which has ruined my hopes of sport this past fortnight. She obliges me to tell you we were all very sorry to hear about the sad discovery at Deane. I remember Mary Ellen. She rode a forward little grey mare that I would have given my eye teeth for. If James could only be persuaded to adopt a rifle and a spaniel, he would not need a kennel. Really, I see no reason why a man needs to ride with hounds when he may take up a gun. Tell our brother, the next time Conker sires a litter, he may have his pick. And tell Father I gave my consent to the dissolution of the trust and advise him to do likewise. True, the lady will find no better return for her capital, but that is her prerogative. Ted is making a dreadful racket and kicking my chair so hard that I am too stupid to compose a charade. Instead, I shall leave off by wishing you all a Merry Christmas and a prosperous New Year.

Best regards,
Ned

PS Don't tell Mother, but Beth will not have turkey on her table, only goose or game. Do send it anyway, and I shall have Cook prepare it to Mother's receipt and bring it directly to my study. But pray make it a small one, as I fear Conker and I will be obliged to finish it by ourselves.

Miss J. Austen
Steventon
Overton
Hants

Chapter Three

Notwithstanding her pledge to her father, Jane considers it most incumbent upon herself to report the details of James's discovery to Lady Isabella at her earliest opportunity. While she has no wish to distress her neighbour unnecessarily, Mary Ellen has been missing for so long. She is presumed dead by all who knew her and must even have been declared so in the eyes of the law so that Mr Chute could take his new bride. Jane is confident the discovery of her skeleton would serve to lessen rather than aggravate Lady Isabella's grief. It would be a tragedy if Mary Ellen's remains were, unwittingly, consigned to a pauper's grave when, after sixteen years' fearing what has become of her errant offspring, it would afford Lady Isabella comfort to lay her to rest. She might even wish to inter her beside her other daughters at Steventon and have Mary Ellen's name added to the memorial.

Jane is sure that Cassandra's pain would have been lessened if her fiancé Mr Fowle's body had been returned to England, rather than buried at sea after he perished of yellow fever off the coast of San Domingo. Having somewhere Cassandra might go to honour her lover might allow her to cherish his memory in peace, rather than sink further into despair as she has done each day since she learned of his death.

And, if Jane's instincts are correct and the remains are those of Mary Ellen, Lady Isabella will no doubt prove vital in identifying them as such. Who could be better placed than a mother to recognize the remains, no matter how decomposed, or the items of clothing they were found wrapped in? Lady Isabella might also provide some insight as to the likelihood of Mary Ellen electing to seek refuge in the cellar, solving the riddle as to whether she went there willingly or was deposited there to conceal the manner of her death. Gaining access to the person of Lady Isabella, however, represents its own challenges. Since the decimation of her family, the wealthy widow spends most of the year abroad, purportedly travelling from one watering place to another in a vain attempt to find relief for her various ailments. Even when she is at home, she welcomes no visitors, attends no social gatherings and does not even set foot out of doors on a Sunday to worship.

Fortunately, Jane is not the only lady determined to seek her out. As a victim of the speckled monster, with a personal fortune of fifty thousand pounds inherited from her father, the earl, Lady Isabella is paramount on Mrs Lefroy's list of desired subscribers to her latest cause. Thus, in seeking to interview Lady Isabella, Jane walks directly past the gated entrance to the park and continues along the lane that leads to St Andrew's church, Ashe. After only a few hundred yards, she intercepts her mark. Mrs Lefroy sits gracefully in the side-saddle, while Lycidas, her faithful bay gelding, puffs out clouds of condensation and plods diligently up the hill. 'Jane, where are you off to on this fine day?'

Indeed, the morning is crisp and bright, and sunlight sparkles from the frost-encrusted leaves of the hedgerow. It is nothing like the December of Jane's birth when, by this date, the persistent snow had risen to meet the rectory gatepost. The winter of 1775 was so severe that birds were liable to freeze on their perches and any livestock left unattended in the exposed fields perished from the cold. Jane, like all her siblings, was christened at home by her father, but Mrs Austen was unable to complete the short walk to St Nicholas's to be churched until the following February, after the snow had melted, further tormenting the valley with floods. On any particularly mild, or severe, day throughout the twenty-two winters since, Mrs Austen has admonished Jane for the freakish conditions that heralded her arrival, as if she were somehow to blame.

'Why, I was on my way to visit you!' she says.

Mrs Lefroy lifts the short veil attached to her sugarloaf hat. 'But I warned you I'd be occupied in soliciting subscriptions this morning.'

Jane must bite her cheek to prevent herself from smiling. 'Then I hope you will allow me the pleasure of accompanying you.'

'Does this mean you've changed your mind about assisting me in ridding the county of the smallpox?' Mrs Lefroy, having recently alighted on a pamphlet by an unknown doctor from Gloucester, has become gripped by the notion she may confer immunity to the disease on all her neighbours.

'In a way . . .' Jane reaches forward to stroke the white star on Lycidas's forehead. Soon after the Lefroys moved to Hampshire, Mrs Lefroy took a keen interest in developing what she calls Jane's 'lively mind' by instructing her reading and encouraging her literary ambitions. Jane is extremely flattered by the attentions of the older, more sophisticated lady, and is aware she is sometimes considered her protégée, but some of Mrs Lefroy's attempts to mould her in her own image carry a little too far. 'How do you go on?'

'Not well at all, I'm afraid. Mr Chute promised me his support, but when I examined the draft he sent me, it was for sixpence. I'm not even sure it's possible to call on a banker for so insignificant an amount. And earlier this morning, Mr Terry all but chased me off his farm and threatened to report me to the magistrate for encouraging disease among his cattle. I fear I will never raise the amount needed to commence. Lady Isabella is my last hope.'

'I don't understand why you need so much money.

Does your scheme involve providing every family with their own infected cow?'

Mrs Lefroy bristles, irritated at Jane's flippancy. 'Did you not read the copy of Dr Jenner's *Inquiry* I loaned you?'

'Upon my honour, I tried. But the illustrations rather upset my constitution, and now Mary has purloined it.' So far as Jane can gather, Dr Jenner believes the smallpox may be avoided by deliberately contracting a malady more usually prevalent in dairy cows and their attendants. However, the only persons to profit from his suggestion thus far are the numerous print-sellers distributing cartoons illustrating the bovine characteristics likely to develop in any subjects brave enough to test his hypothesis.

Mrs Lefroy narrows her eyes. 'For one thing, I need to purchase more pamphlets to convince people to volunteer for the procedure. Especially if you continue to retain my only copy without having the good manners to read it. If I can convince the local landowners, I'm sure their servants and tenants will follow. But even then, the material needs to be collected from the pustule of an infected cow and inserted into a cut while it's fresh. I'll need the use of a carriage, lancets, bandages, perhaps even a surgeon . . .'

Jane recoils. 'Really, it does not sound at all sanitary. Can we not continue with variolation?'

'No, because variolation relies on taking material from a victim of the disease. While it provokes a milder version of the smallpox, even that can prove fatal. Many families are too afraid to subject their children to such a risky procedure, and the poor can hardly afford to miss a day's work while they convalesce. Did your mother have you variolated as a child?'

Jane stares, shamefaced, at the toes of her walking boots. She has not been variolated, as her elder brothers were. After her daughters recovered from typhus, Mrs Austen put off deliberately exposing her children to any more deadly diseases until they had fully recovered their health. For Jane, that day never came. And had Mrs Austen variolated Cassandra or Charles, either might have passed the smallpox, in all its deadly potency, to Jane. 'Very well, you have persuaded me. I shall do my best to help you solicit a generous donation from Lady Isabella. I presume that is who you were on your way to call on?'

Mrs Lefroy raises one arched eyebrow. 'And I suppose that's the only reason I find you loitering nearby the gates of Ashe Park, is it? After previously refusing point blank to lend me your support, or even accompany me on any of my visits to our neighbours?'

'Yes . . .' Jane wavers. It seems Mrs Lefroy knows her too well to accept her sudden change of heart without question. 'Also, if truth be told, I did want to ensure Lady Isabella had been informed about James's grim discovery at the parsonage. I suspect you've heard?'

'There's only one thing that spreads faster than disease, Jane, and that's gossip. But why should Lady

Isabella care about a vagrant soldier who froze to death in your brother's cellar?'

Jane grinds her teeth, infuriated that the magistrate's hasty conclusion is being circulated among her neighbours as established fact. If she does not act swiftly, the truth about whom the remains belonged to and how they came to be concealed below the parsonage will remain buried for ever. 'Because Mr Craven does not have nearly enough evidence to prove, conclusively, that the skeleton belonged to a vagrant soldier. All we know for certain is that the deceased would have disappeared sometime after the winter of 1768 but before the spring of 1783.' She pauses, trusting Mrs Lefroy will be intelligent enough to catch her implication.

'You think it could be Lady Isabella's missing daughter? Oh, Jane! Are you implying someone stole Mary Ellen from her wedding breakfast only to murder her and hide her corpse at Deane?'

'*I* did not say murder. You did!' Jane replies, shocked but not wholly surprised at how quickly Mrs Lefroy's mind turned to violence.

'Then I suppose she might have been hiding there to avoid her new husband, become trapped and starved to death.'

While Jane has considered little else over the last few days, she remains reluctant to voice an opinion. Having fallen prey to her own vivid imagination in the past, she is determined not to fix on a theory until *after* she has investigated all possible avenues. Her priority must be to determine the identity of the corpse beyond any reasonable doubt by persuading Lady Isabella to consider it. True, the head is badly decomposed, but there might be some distinguishing feature that would mark it as her daughter's. Failing that, Jane would very much like to present the white silk garment to Lady Isabella. It could well be the shift or nightgown of a woman of quality and, if it belonged to Mary Ellen, there is a good chance she might recognize it. Mrs Austen can spot her daughters' needlework at a glance. She can even differentiate between Jane and Cassandra's neat stitching – finding them out immediately whenever Cassandra takes over her sister's share of work to provide Jane with more time to further her writing. 'Were you acquainted with Mary Ellen?'

'Not at all. She absconded the Christmas before George was presented with the living of Ashe. The parish was still reeling from the shock when disease broke out and devastated the rest of the family.'

'Poor Lady Isabella, to lose her husband and all her children in such rapid succession,' says Jane. Immediately she can tell, by the guilty expression flitting across the other woman's refined features, that Mrs Lefroy is not wholly sympathetic to the widow. Indeed, part of Jane's motivation in expressing such sentimentality was to encourage any caustic observations her friend might be harbouring.

'Yes, but . . .'

'But?'

'From what I gather, neither Lady Isabella nor Sir Robert could be described as the most devoted of parents. Even before the tragedy, she was rarely at home. Her father was an earl, you know, and before her early marriage, she mixed in the very highest echelons of society. A country seat was never going to be enough to satisfy her self-importance. After she had birthed her three daughters, and it became evident no boy was forthcoming, she set up her own establishment in Town and abandoned her girls to the care of the servants. I warn you, she's an eccentric character. She never conde-scended to receive me until many years after her illness, and that's only because I so doggedly persevered.'

Jane dismisses the temptation to judge Lady Isabella too harshly for the lack of regard she showed her daughters in life. The memorial to Cecilia and Augusta is testament to her love for them. Plus, Jane some-times fears she appreciates more the company of each member of her family, excluding Cassandra, when they are absent from the rectory than when they are present. 'Why did you persevere so?'

'As the wife of a clergyman, I consider it my Christian duty to comfort all those who have been afflicted. Whether by illness or misfortune, it hardly matters. And you know how I enjoy a challenge!' Mrs Lefroy laughs, and Jane knows she is referring to her-self. 'Sincerely, I sometimes fear Lady Isabella mourns the loss of her beauty more than she grieves her family.'

Again, Jane refuses to judge. She does not find it

comfortable to express her vulnerabilities in public and suspects that Lady Isabella's reputedly odd manner is little more than a shield to conceal the extent of her suffering. 'That's as may be, but if there's even the slightest possibility the remains could be Mary Ellen's, her mother has the right to be informed before she is consigned to a pauper's grave. Wouldn't you want to know what had happened if one of your children suddenly disappeared, no matter how terrible the truth?'

At this, Mrs Lefroy looks away, blinking heavily. She has achieved many notable accomplishments over her lifetime, including having several of her poems and articles published, but Jane knows she considers her five living children to be the greatest of all her achievements. Her devotion to their welfare is very likely the reason she looks so coldly on Lady Isabella's maternal failings. 'Very well. Tell Lady Isabella the facts and no more. Do not, under any circumstances, go upsetting her by making any conjectures.'

'As if I would . . .' Jane smiles sweetly. 'Now, how do we find the house? Will I have to climb on Lycidas to pass through the avenue?'

'Oh, no, we'll never get through that way. Follow me through Ashe Farm. Thankfully, her tenant, Mr Bolton, keeps his grounds in a far better state of repair.' Mrs Lefroy clicks her tongue, gently encouraging Lycidas into a graceful trot. Jane proceeds on foot at a distance of several yards behind, most gratified that, so far, this investigation has not necessitated any horseback riding.

Chapter Four

If the grounds of Ashe Park are dishevelled, the Tudor mansion is decrepit. It takes some considerable effort on Mrs Lefroy's part to make their presence known, first by pounding on the door with a fist and then by hallooing through the keyhole, before a ruggedly handsome young manservant, attired in a threadbare livery coat thrown over leather riding breeches, opens it. On being assured that Lady Isabella is expecting them, or expecting Mrs Lefroy at any rate, he leads them through several dank rooms in a highly contemptuous manner.

Jane expects part of his resentment stems from the fact that, despite the mansion being such a grand establishment, he appears to be the only attendant in residence – not allowing for the two fat pugs who relieve themselves in dark corners and tear strips off the carpet as they follow his brisk steps. In the gallery, light patches on the oak panelling indicate where paintings have been removed, and the few pieces of furniture that remain are draped in a protective layer of dust and cobwebs. Ivy adorns the beams overhead. Not, as at Steventon, in honour of the season, but rather because Mother Nature, having extended her reach as far as possible against the exterior of the house, has smashed the panes and crept inside.

They finally arrive at a dingy drawing room, overlooking a tangle of brambles that might once have been a shrubbery, where Lady Isabella receives her visitors. On seeing the tumbled sheets strewn over the chaise longue and the dirty crockery cluttering a nearby card table, Jane suspects she also eats and sleeps there. Mrs Austen would be appalled.

'You may show her in, Wilson. I am dressed . . .' Given the neglected state of her dwelling, Jane had anticipated a morose figure in mourning. Instead, Lady Isabella's trim person is bedecked in a fashionable white gown covered with a short chocolate-brown pelisse, trimmed in turquoise to match her cap and waist-length veil. Her countenance is just about visible beneath heavy turquoise lace as she stands to greet her guests. 'Mrs Lefroy, I see you've brought a companion.'

'Yes, your ladyship. Miss Austen has come to assist in my cause.'

Lady Isabella eyes Jane warily. 'The rector's daughter? I don't believe we've met.'

'No, your ladyship. It's a pleasure to make your acquaintance.' Jane curtseys so low that her knees crack and Lady Isabella's rigid posture softens. She instructs Jane and Mrs Lefroy to sit on a velvet sofa coated in dog hair, without offering them any refreshment. Given the general air of domestic squalor, Jane is glad of it. The room is so chilly, she can see her breath on the air. Perhaps sensing this indication of his dereliction of duty, Wilson picks up a poker and jabs the fire. Under his inexpert attention a half-burned log, which looks suspiciously like the shapely leg of a Queen Anne chair, rolls onto the hearth. He kicks it back into the grate before his mistress notices.

'Come, come, Romulus and Remus.' Lady Isabella clicks her fingers. The pugs shuffle towards her and she blows loud kisses through her veil as she lifts them onto her lap. The portly dogs wriggle and shove each other out of the way to find comfort. It occurs to Jane that she has never made the acquaintance of two beings less likely to survive being raised by wolves. Both are black with grey whiskers around their grumpy little mouths and a bluish sheen to their eyes, indicating they are at least partially blind.

After exchanging their compliments of the season, and a short preamble of Lady Isabella's latest adventures at various watering places (Bath is becoming too crowded, Tunbridge Wells is quite out of fashion, how unfortunate the blockade remains in situ as Vichy is quite delightful in the spring) and the progress of Mrs Lefroy's sons at school (Christopher continues famously, but Benjamin will never master his Latin unless he applies himself), Mrs Lefroy embarks on her mission: 'It's of the utmost importance we act soon.

You'll know, from your own tragic losses, that the disease is most prevalent in the winter months. Indeed, once an outbreak has occurred, it can spread from village to village and take hold across the county in a matter of days. Dr Jenner writes . . .'

'Very well, you may keep your breath to cool your porridge.' Like Jane, Lady Isabella is unwilling to engage in the more venial aspects of Dr Jenner's *Inquiry*. 'My circumstances are rather strained at present, due to the expense of preserving my own health. The various cures my doctors prescribe are not cheap. But I am minded to lend my support to your endeavours and have every expectation of being at liberty to make a contribution very shortly.'

Mrs Lefroy claps her hands. 'Really? That would be splendid.'

'Have you found anything that reverses the effects of the disease?' Jane asks, thinking of Mary. While Mary remains self-conscious of her scars, Jane is glad she is not vain enough to fritter away the family fortune on seeking to restore her beauty or hide behind a lurid veil of turquoise lace.

Lady Isabella raises a bare hand to the firelight. Unlike Mary's, which remain pitted, her blemishes have aged to silver patches. 'Venetian ceruse covers the worst, but my face is still horribly disfigured. I'm afraid I'm quite disgusting under all this lace,' she says, as Wilson scoffs disrespectfully. 'To think there was once a time when I was held up as the most beautiful debutante at

St James, courted by the most eligible bachelors in the country. Even after I had raised my daughters to marriageable age, I was regarded as the most handsome of them all, preferred by several of their suitors. Now, if those same fellows were to see me unveiled, they would recoil in horror.'

'Pray, do not believe so, Lady Isabella,' says Mrs Lefroy. 'This awful disease has cursed such a high proportion of the population that, really, a countenance such as yours is not at all uncommon. You must not allow your affliction to deprive you of society, or to deprive society of your presence.'

'Oh, but you would not understand. Only a woman who has possessed great beauty can imagine the pain of losing it,' Lady Isabella replies, as Jane is forced to choke on her laughter. Among their neighbours, Mrs Lefroy is considered a remarkably elegant woman. Although clearly not by Lady Isabella's exacting standards. 'And added to my ruined complexion, my constitution is frail. The slightest interaction fatigues me. Rest is really the only restorative.' She looks pointedly at the chaise longue. 'So, if that's all?'

Jane takes a deep breath. 'There is another matter you should be aware of.'

'Yes?'

'There's been a discovery at Deane Parsonage. You may have heard that my brother, the clergyman, had the misfortune to uncover human remains in the cellar.'

'Wilson mentioned there had been some talk at the

Wheatsheaf Inn about a deceased soldier . . .' Lady Isabella replies, her tone wary. 'But I do not see why such a matter would concern me.'

'Well, the magistrate has concluded the corpse is that of a vagrant soldier . . . but, having been present at the discovery, I do not think we can know that for certain. True, it was wrapped in a regimental jacket, but that wasn't the only item of clothing present, and no other military paraphernalia was found. Added to that, I strongly believe the skeleton is too slight to be that of a full-grown man. All that is certain is that it belonged to someone who would have died after 1768 but before the spring of 1783.' Jane pauses, but Lady Isabella does not flinch. 'I'm sure, if you appealed to my brother, he could arrange for you to examine the remains.'

'Why should I wish to do such a ghastly thing?'

Jane looks to Mrs Lefroy for assistance, but she simply frowns. On this brief summation of the facts, Mr Austen, Mrs Lefroy and even Mary had all intuited that Jane was suggesting the remains could be Mary Ellen's. Lady Isabella, however, appears unwilling to consider the possibility. Jane will need to dispense with any delicacy of feeling. 'Forgive me, ma'am, but in case it is your daughter.'

Lady Isabella turns her face to the side, revealing her sharp profile. 'Impossible. All my daughters are accounted for in the crypt of St Nicholas's church.'

'B-but I was led to understand that one went missing and was never found?'

'You are referring, I expect, to Mary Ellen?'

'Yes.' Jane nods.

'That wretched girl ceased to be my daughter from the moment she elected to flee this house. She was born to torment me and has been as good as dead to me these past sixteen years already.'

Jane is caught off guard by Lady Isabella's vitriol. While she might have anticipated that Mary Ellen's decision to abandon her new husband would have caused an estrangement between herself and her parents, Jane had assumed her subsequent fate, and the diminishment of the rest of her family, would have induced some pity in her mother by now. 'Even so, are you not concerned as to what became of her?'

'Not at all. Why should I be? She certainly did not concern herself with her obligations to me. She threw off her affiliations to this family when she humiliated us so publicly and defied our wishes and expectations for her future. Oh, and after I had worked tirelessly to persuade Mr Chute to take her.'

'It certainly was a tragedy,' Jane replies, noting Lady Isabella seems more offended by the social disgrace than her daughter's unhappiness. If she cannot yet enlist her help in identifying the remains, she must at least probe her on the circumstances of Mary Ellen's disappearance. 'She must have given you her reasons for objecting so violently to the match?'

'Object?' Lady Isabella splutters. 'I did not ask for the chit's opinion. She was nothing but an awkward country girl of sixteen, without education or even beauty to recommend her,' she says, seemingly unaware that Mary Ellen's lack of education shows as much failing on her part as on her daughter's. 'And yet she could have been mistress of The Vyne! A remarkable fate for such an ill-formed creature. My one consolation in bringing such a plain, obstinate girl into the world would have been to see her established so. Did you know the gentlemen I had in mind for Cecilia and Augusta cried off after Mary Ellen's disgrace? No one could be persuaded to take my remaining daughters off my hands, after their sister behaved so abominably. A Miss Portal could not be relied upon to keep her marriage vows.'

One of the many questions Jane has about Mary Ellen's disappearance is why she absconded *after* becoming Mrs Chute. If she left of her own accord, surely it would have been preferable to do so before being yoked to a husband she did not care for. 'But Mary Ellen went through with the ceremony?'

'She had no choice but to do so. From the moment she learned of the arrangement, I kept her locked in her room, separated even from her sisters. Do not look so horrified, Miss Austen. My design was simply to make her so uncomfortable that she would be grateful for her new position. I only wish I had paid her such attentions earlier, so she might have learned to be a more dutiful daughter. But my husband refused my demands that all three girls be sent away to school at the earliest opportunity. He feared the expense of an education would be wasted on daughters and, instead, allowed them to remain here in idle insolence. Really, I warned him it would not end well. We should have expected no better from a young miss who'd been allowed to run wild for the first fifteen years of her life. Your father presided over the ceremony, you know.'

'I did not,' replies Jane, wondering why Mr Austen had not told her of this. Probably to prevent her from investigating the matter further by interrogating him. 'At St Nicholas's?'

'Yes, and afterwards every respectable family in the county and beyond assembled here for the wedding breakfast. The gallery was festooned in ribbons and Christmas roses. When Mary Ellen could not be found to stand up with her new husband, we assumed she had retired to her bedchamber to change her clothes. But after Mr Chute became increasingly impatient for his bride, I sent Cecilia to retrieve her and, to our dismay, we discovered she had fled.'

'Why are you so certain she left of her own accord?' asks Jane. If the house was as crowded as Lady Isabella claims, it is possible someone might have abducted Mary Ellen from her own home.

'She left a note, tossed upon her bed beside her ruined bouquet. In it, the stupid, illiterate girl declared she would rather work for her bread than be a wife. Well, may she have her wish. Let her live out her days as a contemptible governess or a lady's companion. She will never see a penny of my fortune.'

Due to the nature of Lady Isabella's housekeeping, Jane sincerely doubts there will be a stick of furniture left, or that Ashe Park will even remain standing, by the time she dies. 'And no one disappeared at the same time as her? She might have been accompanied by a sweetheart, perhaps?'

'Ha! Mary Ellen had no beaux. She was positively green. Her world went as far as the dairy to the north and the church to the south.'

Despite Lady Isabella's assurances, Jane makes a note to question whoever she can about Mary Ellen's friendships, young ladies of sixteen being perhaps the most practised at concealing unsuitable attachments from their mothers. She may have been tethered to the estate, but perhaps she was on more than cordial terms with a groom. Or an officer stationed nearby, given the coat the corpse was found wrapped in. 'My brother remembered her as a horsewoman. Did you check your stables to see if any of the mounts were missing?'

'Of course. It was the first place Sir Robert searched. But all the horses, including her pony, were accounted for.'

Jane nods. Mary Ellen's only hope of escaping the neighbourhood on foot and alone would have been to catch the stagecoach from Deane Gate Inn. Perhaps she was on her way there when she was waylaid and somehow ended up concealed beneath the parsonage. 'And you've never heard from her, in all this time?'

'I warned her I would not forgive her if she defied

my attempts to secure her future, and I never have.'

Even the tragic death of Lady Isabella's husband and both her other daughters has not abated her ire towards Mary Ellen. Surely, by now, her fury should have been spent. Jane's own mother is not the most patient or outwardly affectionate parent, but Jane cannot imagine what terrible act she would have to commit for Mrs Austen to cut all ties with her for ever. 'But what if, after being persuaded to leave your care, she died at the hands of some dastardly villain and was left to moulder in that cellar?'

'Jane!' exclaims Mrs Lefroy. 'I do apologize, your ladyship.'

'Miss Austen, Mary Ellen may be lost to me but I've no doubt she is alive and well and living the miserable life she deserves after abandoning her station.' Beneath her veil, Lady Isabella's eyes narrow. 'It was Mr Chute who had her declared dead so that he could remarry. Now, Mrs Lefroy, I'd be grateful if you could take your impudent companion and leave me in peace.'

'Of course, ma'am.' Mrs Lefroy's fingers close around Jane's wrist.

'I told you not to upset her,' she hisses in Jane's ear, as they depart under the malicious gaze of Wilson and the pugs.

But, Jane fears, Lady Isabella was not upset – not at the fate of Mary Ellen. What kind of cold, unnatural mother could show no curiosity as to the whereabouts of her last remaining daughter, even if estranged? Is it the hope that Mary Ellen lives that encourages Lady Isabella to insist she remains missing rather than dead? Or is there a more sinister reason she wishes everyone to believe she is still alive? Only one thing is certain: if Mary Ellen's mother will not investigate what became of her, then Jane must.

LETTER 4

From Miss Jane Austen to Miss Austen

Steventon, 22 December 1798

My dearest Cassandra,

Would you believe Lady Isabella pretends no curiosity as to the fate of her missing daughter? I fear, if one of Mother's children perished in such mysterious circumstances, even if it was due to our own misadventure, she would make a point of locating us expressly to berate our bones for our folly. But, seriously, how can her ladyship possess no desire to comprehend the identity of the remains discovered at Deane? Is it because she is already privy to the circumstances of Mary Ellen's demise? Could a mother, excessively provoked by a daughter's disobedience, go so far as to murder her and conceal her corpse? Sixteen years have passed since the scandal arose, but Lady Isabella remains as full of spite as she must have been on the day Mary Ellen absconded. What a proud, vengeful creature she is. I see no need for her to hide herself away when her countenance cannot be any more blighted than Mary's. But, then, Mary tells me there are two varieties of the smallpox and, as you might expect, she claims to have had the better sort.

If Lady Isabella will not assist in my enquiries, I shall proceed to question Mary Ellen's other known acquaintances – beginning with her jilted groom, Mr Chute. You see, I really am appreciative of Elizabeth Chute's kind invitation to The Vyne and my costume for the Children's Ball is coming along splendidly. So much so that by Christmas Eve I shall be adorned for battle. You are relieved from signing the white turkey's death warrant. Mother feared it would not be large enough to feed the party at Godmersham, and thus I encouraged her to wave the black spotted gobbler off on the stage this morning. Pray ask Beth how many full courses of exquisite dishes she intends to convert it into. Tell her my mother is all anticipation.

Yours graciously,
J.A.

PS Whip Teddy for me and tell him not to kick chairs so that I might receive nice long letters from Godmersham.

Miss Austen
Edward Austen's Esqr
Godmersham Park
Faversham
Kent

LETTER 5

From Lieutenant Charles Austen to Miss Jane Austen

HMS Scorpion, *North Sea, 1 December 1798*

Dear Jane,

I could not for the life of me recall whether you asked for black or red stockings, so I took the liberty of purchasing two pairs of each (as I know you would not forget Cassy). Pray tell me you have not spent the money you put aside for this commission, as I was forced to borrow the extra. Likewise, I do not know whether to wish you many happy returns, merry Christmas or a happy new year as by the time you receive this it could well be Whitsun and you another year older.

It's very hard to have Christmas without a ball. In calmer waters, the captain takes out his fiddle and we practise our steps. The midshipmen are not as pretty as the girls in Southampton, but they are less discerning as to whom they stand up with. If you are so fortunate as to be invited to a dance in Hampshire, do not sit down once. Dance every set as if your poor brother's life depended on it and then send me a list of your partners so that I may imagine you in high spirits and keep Christmas with my family in my breast. Which reminds me to task you with my charade:

My first is in harvest rarely known,
Nor would it welcome be.
My next in country or in town,
Each miss delights to see.
And when drear winter's dress is shown,
In joyous play my whole is thrown.

Your own particular little brother,
Charles

LLABWONS SI REWSNA EHT SP
PPS I have made a friend of the ship's cat by offering her my scraps and she is entering into the spirit of the season by bringing me gifts. I will not offer to share her spoils with you, as I do not think you would like them. Do you remember the time Cassy was taken by surprise by a perfectly preserved mouse in her workbox? Oh, how we laughed!

Miss J. Austen
Steventon
Overton
Hants

Chapter Five

In the days leading up to Christmas Eve, Jane scrutinizes the Steventon parish register and finds William Chute of Sherborne and Mary Ellen Portal of Ashe were 'Married in St Nicholas's Church, by Licence on the Fifteenth Day of December in the Year One Thousand Seventeen Hundred and Eighty-Two', by the Reverend George Austen, and in the presence of Lady Isabella and Sir Robert Portal, third baronet.

It was sobering to find Mary Ellen's looping signature in the register, knowing her hand had been forced. This small testament, scratched in ink, seems the only tangible mark Mary Ellen ever left. Since her disappearance, the living, breathing girl has become no more than a shadowy apparition or cautionary tale.

When Jane questioned her father as to why he had not mentioned his involvement in her ill-fated union, he replied, rather testily, that as a clergyman of almost thirty years, he had presided over scores, if not hundreds, of such ceremonies and could not be expected to recall the particulars of each. Furthermore, it is not for the rector to deduce whether both parties come to the altar freely or shoulder the blame for any subsequent breakdown of their marriage. Really, Mr Austen had enough concerns of his own at the time – what with the constant demands of providing for a growing family, eking a living out of his glebe lands and attending to the spiritual welfare of his flock. Why, even if he did recall his role in the event, he saw no reason to mention it to Jane as, apart from her wild imaginings, there is nothing to suggest the remains found at Deane are those of the runaway bride.

Despite his protests, or perhaps because of them, Jane suspects the reason for her father's reticence is guilt over whatever happened to Mary Ellen directly after she left his church. Undeterred by his obfuscation, she determines to press ahead with her plans to interview Mr Chute. This will involve Jane breaking the Austen tradition of spending Christmas Eve by the rectory fireside, puzzling over charades composed by the family, but, since she has already solved James and Charles's efforts, Neddy refuses to comply, and Henry, Frank and Cassandra's are yet to arrive, this will be no great loss and may even serve to distract her from lamenting the absence of so many of her siblings. Added to this, her father cannot censure her enquiries at the ball as Mr and Mrs Austen conveniently declined the invitation, citing their advanced years and the intemperate weather, rather than admit to the truth of their general disinclination for anyone's company but their own. Instead, James has kindly agreed to convey her thither.

Initially, Mary could not be persuaded to release him, not even to oblige his sister as, much to her chagrin, she is barred from partaking in any such merriment until she agrees to be churched. However, with the frost refusing to thaw until ever later in the afternoon, Mary prefers to keep to her bed, being fed caudle at regular intervals by the increasingly flustered Rosalee. Even after Jane reminded her that, as Mr Chute is James's patron in the church, it was his duty to attend, she was not minded to part with her husband. It was not until Mrs Austen pointed out that, as the occasion was expressly billed as a Children's Ball, James could take Anna too, Mary condescended to release him. Alas, Jane fears that since giving birth to her own child, Mary's already tepid affections towards her step-daughter have cooled even further. Of late, she seems to have even less patience for Anna's noisy play and grows visibly alarmed when the little girl asks to cuddle her new brother.

Thus, it lifts Jane's heart to see her niece, dressed as St Lucy in her best white frock with a crown of evergreens and four candles, which Mrs Austen has wisely cautioned are to remain unlit, set upon her head as she bounces along the bench beside her with glee. The little girl's eyes stretch even wider as the carriage turns sharply from the road and along the short avenue to reach the scene of the much-anticipated festivities.

The former Tudor palace is the principal home in the neighbourhood and, in its three-hundred-year history, has accommodated various royals, including King Henry VIII and two of his ill-fated queens, Catherine of Aragon and Anne Boleyn. Today frost settles on its expansive clay roof and intricately patterned brickwork, making it appear that the magnificent house has been showered with diamonds. Ice gathers around the edges of a glassy lake, set before the classic portico of the north front, so that it may better admire the grandeur of its own reflection. In the furthest reaches of the east wing, exquisite stained-glass windows mark the family's private chantry chapel, used exclusively to pray for the souls of the dead. Jane wonders if Mary Ellen's name is ever included in those prayers.

They alight, under the protective gaze of a giant fir tree, and Jane clasps Anna's hand tightly as they are ushered inside by a duo of bewigged footmen. The imperial staircase is clothed in branches of holly, its red berries bright against the dazzling white plasterwork and highly polished marble busts of Roman emperors. To be mistress of The Vyne would be something indeed, and Jane can sympathize with any mother coveting such an elevated position for her daughter.

With time and suffering, Lady Isabella has soured into a spiteful creature, but her original motivations in prevailing on Mary Ellen to accept Mr Chute's suit may not have been unkind. Especially as she herself was reputedly married to advantage at an early age. Any mother of three girls would be conscious that a good marriage was the best way of securing their future. Even when young ladies are set to inherit, it is not unreasonable for their families to expect them to acquire more. If Mr Chute had had a son of marriageable age, Mrs Austen would have been herding Jane and Cassandra towards him with all the subtlety of a sheepdog.

In the long oak gallery, an enormous yuletide log burns bright as swarms of footmen hand out crystal tumblers of Negus, scenting the air with nutmeg and cinnamon. Amid the revelry, Jane is most amused by the disguises her neighbours have thrown together, fulfilling Mrs Chute's theme of fairy tales and folk heroes to varying degrees. She herself has chosen elegance over amusement and has fashioned a Mameluke cap and robe à *la turque* from her former blue petticoat in honour of Nelson's victory on the Nile. James, who protested a costume would be an affront to his dignity as a clergyman, consented only to the addition of his father's peruke and frock coat, so that he appears a relic from an earlier era. Likewise, Mr Chute seems to be reminiscing over his youth, by presenting himself as Queen Elizabeth's roguish courtier Sir Walter Raleigh. 'Will you be joining the hunt?' he asks James, over the frill of his starched ruff, by way of greeting.

'I would not miss it, sir,' replies James, who had faithfully promised his wife, only an hour earlier, that in recompense for deserting her on Christmas Eve, he would spend St Stephen's Day at home this year.

As the two men continue to converse with great enthusiasm about dogs and horses, Jane watches the old man carefully. He is small and sprightly, and she has only ever known him to display violence when on the sporting field. Despite this, she forces herself to consider what motivation he could possibly have had for dispensing with his first wife. Lady Isabella claimed Mary Ellen left a note proving her removal from Ashe Park was of her own accord. But, without seeing it, Jane will not dismiss the possibility it may have been forged. Perhaps Mary Ellen rejected her new husband's advances directly after the ceremony, causing him to fly into a temper. Most young ladies are too well bred to risk incivility in public but, in private, it may have proved impossible for Mary Ellen to hide her revulsion. And, if Mr Chute was not aware of her disinclination to marry him, the coolness of her disposition towards him may have come as a shock. Affianced couples from good families are rarely left alone together long enough to measure each other's character. Perhaps, rather than immodesty, it is this very outcome such laws of decorum seek to prevent – for how many marriages would take place if the true nature of one's potential spouse could be known in advance?

'Come along, little one.' Jane's friend Alethea Bigg, scandalously clad in a pair of her younger brother's yellow leather riding breeches, her auburn hair arranged as ears, and a tail pinned to her rear, steps forward to peel Anna away from Jane's knee. 'We're getting up a game of blind man's buff. You won't want to miss it!' Further inside the long gallery, Mr Bigg-Wither, Alethea's father, has donned a cocked hat and is ringing a bell in the manner of a town crier while several children hang onto his tailcoats. It takes Jane a moment to realize the pair are meant to be Dick Whittington, as Lord Mayor of London, and his cat.

'No need to be shy.' Jane gently encourages her niece to join the fray, trusting that Alethea and Mr Bigg-Wither will preside over a far milder version of the game than the Austen boys engaged in at the rectory. There, as soon as a length of ribbon was wound tight around the hapless blind man's eyes, the brothers would rearrange the furniture so that he could not fail to trip. Eventually, Mr Austen had to ban the game as sport only for the bonesetter.

'Today would have been a fine day to ride out with the hounds,' Mr Chute continues, to James's hearty agreement.

Usually, Jane is not so ill-mannered as to attend a Christmas gathering only to accuse the host of murder, but she knows this may be her only opportunity to gauge Mr Chute's reaction to the possible re-emergence of his first wife. Lady Isabella had claimed Mr Chute's motive for having Mary Ellen declared dead was pecuniary but, by removing Mary Ellen before they began their married life in earnest, he would have risked Sir Robert pressing to have the union annulled and dissolving his daughter's settlement. From what

Jane has witnessed of Mr Chute's affairs previously, he is far too shrewd to have allowed for such an eventuality, but what a man does when he is in a temper is not always rational. If he did kill her, the discovery of her remains will surely rattle him. And if Lady Isabella or Sir Robert was responsible for Mary Ellen's death, he may prove a vital witness. 'Did James mention the sad discovery at Deane Parsonage?'

'The corpse?' Mr Chute nods. 'Yes, very shocking.'

'Only he thinks there's a possibility it could be Mary Ellen.'

'Jane!' James rushes to defend himself. 'I said no such thing.'

'*My* Mary Ellen,' Mr Chute's rheumy eyes glimmer, as if Jane has mentioned passing a long-lost acquaintance on the road. 'Could it really?'

'I very much doubt it, sir,' says James. 'In fact, Mr Craven was confident the deceased was a vagrant soldier. You see, I found it wrapped in a regimental coat.'

'But with no boots, or other items of military wear,' Jane adds, before Mr Chute's shoulders sag too far in disappointment. 'Also we've ascertained it must have appeared after our family vacated in 1768 but before the Lloyds took possession in 1783. And, really, the remains were so slight, they could only have been those of a boy or a woman.'

Mr Chute blinks. 'But Deane Parsonage, what would Mary Ellen have been doing there?' Even Jane must concede, if her new husband had killed her, it would have been quite an undertaking to remove Mary Ellen's body from Ashe to Deane without any of the wedding party noticing, and take some considerable effort to feign surprise when she could not be located. If Mr Chute really did bear any resentment towards his bride, it would have been far more convenient to take her home and murder her in private. Or, as is the wont of some malicious husbands, keep her alive only to inflict misery on her for the rest of her days.

'We cannot possibly say, sir. Was she upset at all on the morning of your wedding?' asks Jane, as James stares daggers at her. 'Overcome with emotion at the gravity of the moment, perhaps?'

'Not at all. She was always a very composed, dignified young lady. Really, her disappearance remains a terrible mystery.'

'Mr Craven believes that whoever it was likely sheltered in the cellar for warmth – and froze to death,' says James, anxious to dispel any hint that Jane may be accusing his patron of wrongdoing.

Mr Chute takes a sharp breath. 'But I had the militia scour the woods. There was no trace of her.'

'The militia?' Perhaps Mr Austen was right in his initial assessment, and Mary Ellen had run off with a soldier – only to be betrayed in the worst way imaginable. Or she might have come across one while making her escape, and thereby met her demise. 'Was a regiment stationed nearby at the time?'

'The Buckinghamshires were marching to Portsmouth, ready to fight in the colonial uprising. I paid the commander a handsome fee to have his men join the search, and they scoured the woods for five days and nights. I even took my hounds out searching for her. If she had lost her way, or was hiding hereabouts, I was sure one of the pack would pick up her scent but they could find no trace of her beyond the estate.'

'Did you examine the parsonage?' If Mary Ellen was not murdered, either by her parents or her new husband, her determination to remain hidden from the search party could have been her downfall. Perhaps Jane should try climbing into the cellar and closing the hatch after herself to test whether it is possible to open it again from the inside. The thought of becoming hopelessly trapped in such a confined space makes the hairs on her arms stand up. She will ask James to do it instead.

'I assume so, if it was empty at that time. Have you shared your suspicions with Lady Isabella?'

'Indeed, sir. I told her myself.'

'She admitted you?'

'Myself and Mrs Lefroy.'

Mr Chute looks more shocked at this revelation than he did at the possible discovery of his first wife's skeleton. 'And did she give any clue as to whether she might attend today?'

'No, sir. We did not discuss the ball.'

'Never mind, I shall try calling on her again. Tell me,

was there anything else found with the skeleton that led you to believe it might possibly be Mary Ellen?'

James opens his mouth to decline, but Jane speaks over him. 'Some other scraps of fabric – including what I believe was once a very fine white silk. I was hoping Lady Isabella might at least agree to examine the remains, but she was most adamant that she would not.'

'I'll see what can be done to persuade her,' says Mr Chute. 'And, in the meantime, I should like to inspect them myself, and the site of their discovery. Unless they've already been buried?'

James shoots Jane a reproving glance, all too aware of the horrors to which she has persuaded Mr Chute to expose himself. 'Not yet, sir. The ground has been too hard to dig. But I must warn you, it is not a pleasant sight.'

'I understand that, but I fear it's my duty. And it would be of great comfort to myself and, no doubt, Lady Isabella, to lay Mary Ellen to rest, at last. If we are able to find any clue it was her, then I would gladly inter her here. Our marriage may have been brief, but I would not have my wife buried in a pauper's grave.'

'A very noble sentiment, sir.' Jane nods her approval, satisfied that Mr Chute seems willing to do all that is proper towards his missing bride. Although she does not think it would be appropriate to inter Mary Ellen beside the Chutes for all eternity – given she most likely died in her attempt to avoid becoming one of the family. 'And if you could persuade Lady Isabella to reconsider her decision, I expect she may prove even more helpful.' If Mr Chute was guilty of murdering Mary Ellen, Jane sincerely doubts he'd be so willing to entertain the possibility that the remains belonged to her, or to entangle himself in the affair at all.

'Oh, Mr Chute!' Mrs Lefroy, disguised as a demurely dressed Amazon, calls from across the room. 'I think there has been a mistake with the banker's draft you gave me.'

'Do excuse me. I must make sure my kitchen has prepared enough white soup.' The old man scampers away, hotly pursued by Mrs Lefroy clutching her bow and arrow to her side.

As he does so, Jane's eye alights on Mr Chute's present wife. Perhaps, to get a real understanding of how he behaves behind closed doors, Jane should be questioning her.

Chapter Six

At the opposite end of the long oak gallery, the second Mrs Chute is taking the opportunity of fancy dress to expose even more of herself than usual. Dressed as a milkmaid, with a tightly laced bodice, short petticoats and a pail fashioned from chip set upon her head, she is the romantic ideal of pastoral impracticability. As Jane weaves through the assembled party of overexcited children to reach her, her only dilemma is how she will persuade Mrs Chute to confide in her when, by tacit agreement, they usually make every effort to avoid each other.

The present mistress of The Vyne is fonder of Jane's brothers' company than of hers, and Jane would prefer to forgo company altogether than resort to that of Mrs Chute. After the humiliation of losing Mary Ellen on their wedding day, most had assumed that Mr Chute would remain a widower for life. Many eyebrows were raised, therefore, when, approaching his dotage, he brought home his lively and handsome second wife. Especially as the couple appear to be so ill-suited. Mr

Chute's interests extend only so far as sport and amassing wealth, whereas his wife's revolve chiefly around causing all the young men of the county to fall in love with her. Jane has long suspected James of being in her thrall, and she is certainly fond of him.

Despite marrying Mary, James has a weakness for aristocratic women: his first wife, Anne, was the granddaughter of a duke. Whereas, Jane suspects, Mrs Chute's preference for her brother may have sprung from no other foundation than, as vicar of St John's, Sherborne, and a dedicated sportsman, he is one of the very few visitors received with any regularity at The Vyne.

A footman presents a tidy stack of hand-painted cards arranged face down on a silver tray. A spark of excitement runs through Jane's veins. The pack will have been designed for frivolity rather than gambling. 'Care to draw a character, miss?'

'Indeed!' Jane swipes the entire deck before the bemused footman can object. As anticipated, each portrays a caricature, which the bearer must enter into with spirit so that others might guess their identity without being shown the card. As she waits for Mrs Chute to finish greeting her guests, Jane shuffles the deck until she finds her favourite, Madame Candour, and places it face down on the very top. 'Shall we play?'

'Oh!' Mrs Chute startles at the unusual sensation of being accosted by Jane. She shuffles to the right and then to the left, desperately trying to make her escape, but Jane matches her panicked steps with the skill of a fencing master. Unfortunately for Jane's prey, the oak gallery is the longest room at The Vyne – nay, in England – and there is only one exit, which currently stands at more than eighty feet away. Realizing she is trapped, Mrs Chute draws the carefully placed top card. 'As you insist.' She glances at it and, lacking any imagination of her own, arranges a golden curl over her naked shoulder as she waits for Jane to commence.

'I do hope I have not distressed your husband, when he has been so kind as to host us. I fear I may have raised a most indelicate topic.'

'Unless you bring news of his bank failing, or the mange breaking out in his kennels, you'll have had little chance of ruffling my husband's feathers.'

Excellent. Mrs Chute has clearly taken the bait and is eager for Jane to guess her character immediately so that she may bestow her company on her other guests. 'Even more indelicate than that, I'm afraid. I expect you've heard of my brother's macabre discovery at Deane,' Mrs Chute nods warily. 'Well, without intending to alarm Mr Chute, I felt obliged to raise the possibility that the remains might be those of your predecessor, his first wife, Mary Ellen . . .'

'Then, please, do not concern yourself on my husband's account.' Mrs Chute tips her head back and drains her glass before continuing. 'He never gave a fig for Mary Ellen.'

Jane is taken aback by the bitterness of her tone.

That is not the story of the desperate jilted groom she has been told and retold over many a yuletide log. And Mr Chute seemed genuinely moved by her mention of Mary Ellen. He is the only person, other than Jane, who is willing to entertain the notion that the skeleton might be hers. He even volunteered to put himself through the ordeal of examining the severely decomposed remains, and to persuade Lady Isabella to do likewise. 'He did not?'

'No. It was Lady Isabella's affection he sought to gain by attaching himself to her daughter.'

'Mr Chute was in love with Lady Isabella?' Jane echoes, in disbelief. This is a complication she had not foreseen. But as the lady herself was so keen to boast, prior to her illness she was considered so beautiful that her daughters' suitors often admired her charms over theirs. Is this the reason Mary Ellen disappeared? Could she have discovered her new husband's partiality to her mother on her wedding day and fled the house in mortification? It would be preferable to be slighted for any other woman in the world than one's own mother. Thankfully, with Mrs Austen's sharp temper and low tolerance for fools, it is not a fate that Jane can imagine befalling herself or Cassandra.

'He still is. What do you think all this is in aid of?' Mrs Chute waves one white arm around the crowded gallery. 'He never permits me to entertain. Every time I suggest opening The Vyne, he rails against having his hospitality abused. But when I proposed a masquerade, he finally relented. No doubt because he hoped *she* might attend in a costume to conceal her frightful countenance.'

Lady Isabella, in her lurid lace veil, would not look out of place among the assembled company. Several of the guests have opted to cover their faces: Mrs Rivers is dressed as Red Riding Hood, while her daughter, Clara, is presumably the Big Bad Wolf in a papier-mâché mask and bedraggled fur tippet. Yet it would seem a foolish move to marry the daughter to secure the mother. Mr Chute would have known that, after marrying Mary Ellen, the law would never allow him to take Lady Isabella as a wife. Even if there was to come a time when they were both single, such a union would remain incest in the eyes of the law. But perhaps, like his wife, Mr Chute does not object to seeking affection outside matrimony. 'His bride's own mother? Are you certain?'

'Why do you think he refrained from having the marriage annulled after Mary Ellen disappeared?'

'Because he was hoping she would return?'

'So, you're a romantic, are you, Miss Austen?' Mrs Chute looks down her long nose at Jane in a manner so withering it could melt ice.

'To keep her dowry, then?'

She shakes her head, causing her pail to wobble precariously. 'There was no dowry to speak of. Lady Isabella retains a lifetime interest in Ashe Park, but the estate is entailed.'

'But surely her parents awarded her something upon

her marriage?' Jane cannot imagine Mr Chute, even in his younger days, being tempted to marry without fortune.

'When Lady Isabella married Sir Robert, the earl granted her fifty thousand pounds to be managed by a board of trustees to prevent it from being swallowed by her husband's estate, which, upon her death, was to be divided equally among her children. That's all the Portal girls would ever have been entitled to, providing they outlived her. But as soon as Mary Ellen fled, Lady Isabella persuaded the late earl to transfer it to a new trust, the beneficiaries of which were to be Cecilia and Augusta only.'

'Lady Isabella *cut out* Mary Ellen before attempting to find out what had become of her?' Jane could tell from Lady Isabella's cold demeanour that she held little maternal affection for her daughter, but to write her out of her will in the days following her disappearance seems most rash. Is this what Lady Isabella meant when she stated Mary Ellen had been dead to her these sixteen years already? Whether Mary Ellen continued to draw breath or not, her mother and her lawyers had already struck her from the family line.

'She was so incensed at her disobedience that she disinherited her immediately. Even if Mary Ellen had reappeared, begging her mother's and her husband's forgiveness for running away, Lady Isabella was adamant she would never reinstate her in her affections or her will. More than that, she would not risk her daughter outliving her, then reappearing to claim her fortune after her demise.' Mrs Chute pauses, allowing Jane to consider her revelations. An inheritance from her mother would have been Mary Ellen's only chance of independence. If Mr Chute had annulled the marriage, and she had one day been able to step forward and claim her portion, she might have led a modest but respectable life. Perhaps this was the outcome she was hoping for when she fled her wedding breakfast. 'I know because my husband was one of the trustees. His interest was declared in our marriage settlement. He impoverished his own wife to appease Lady Isabella. That is how I can be absolutely certain he preferred mother over daughter.'

'Then why, as you say, did he remain married to Mary Ellen rather than having their union annulled?' Given there was no pecuniary advantage to remaining married to Mary Ellen after her public desertion, it is odd that Mr Chute did not throw her off immediately. As they had yet to spend one evening together as man and wife before she disappeared, it would not have been difficult for him to argue the marriage had not been consummated.

Mrs Chute huffs with impatience. She is probably wondering why the famously astute Jane is failing to guess her character, despite her candour bordering on offence. 'To remain tight with the family. Being Lady Isabella's son-in-law gave him an acceptable motive to call on Lady Isabella. Before her illness, they would spend many hours closeted in her dressing room, comforting each other on their mutual humiliation. Now, the only reason she remains in correspondence with him is to draw the interest from her trust. But, since the bond has matured and Lady Isabella is a widow, she seeks to dissolve the arrangement and gain control of the capital herself. My husband fears he will be forced to relinquish her once and for all.'

Jane recalls Neddy's letter: *And tell Father I gave my consent to the dissolution of the trust and advise him to do likewise. True, the lady will find no better return for her capital, but that is her prerogative.* Could Jane's family have been complicit in stripping Mary Ellen of her fortune as well as solemnizing the union that sealed her fate? 'How cruel of Mary Ellen's own mother to have cast her aside before she could be certain what had become of her.'

'Such is the way with us great families. A legacy must be passed on to one who will preserve it.' Mrs Chute fiddles with the ribbons on her bodice as she betrays the rationale behind her own marriage. As she had thirty thousand pounds, and Mr Chute was a childless widower with a vast estate to pass on, Jane expects the compatibility of their characters was neither here nor there in drawing up the arrangements. He will have been looking for a wife young enough to bear him an heir, while her father would have sought to marry her to a man rich enough to protect her interests. 'I suppose, having no fortune, you will be permitted to marry for love?'

Jane fights desperately to keep her face placid. At twenty-three, she is beginning to wonder if she will marry at all, let alone for love. 'At least your father did you the kindness of choosing a husband you are likely to outlive.'

'Are you Madame Candour too?' Mrs Chute narrows her eyes at the forgotten card in Jane's hand. 'The stationer promised me there were no duplicates in this pack.'

Realizing she has tested Mrs Chute's character to its limits, without making the slightest attempt to enter into her own, Jane lets out a note so high it may shatter the crystal tumblers of Negus. The party pauses momentarily to admire her efforts, before proffering a round of applause.

'Very clever. Good evening, Madame Top Note. Now if you'll excuse me, I must see to my other guests.'

As Mrs Chute accosts a rather dashing young gentleman disguised as a highwayman, with a handkerchief knotted over his face, Jane breaks the deck of cards into two then fans them together. It seems to her that Mary Ellen's life has been snuffed out thrice – first when her mother struck her from her will, second when Mr Chute had her legally declared dead, and finally when she was left to moulder in the cellar of Deane Parsonage. Could it really have been so easy to make an inconvenient young lady disappear? Did Mr Chute agree to impoverish his wife, and by turns himself, because he knew Mary Ellen was already dead and would therefore never inherit? Or did Lady Isabella, having sought to remove Mary Ellen from her hands by marriage, resort to more extreme means to rid herself of the daughter she described as being 'born to torment' her? After interviewing the two living persons meant to have been closest to Mary Ellen, Jane fears she is yet to identify anyone who truly cared for her. Her heart aches for a young woman sorely betrayed by those who should have loved her. On the long carriage ride home, through the bitterly cold night, Jane can almost hear Mary Ellen's spirit calling from the woods, urging her to discover the truth so that she may finally rest in peace.

LETTER 6

From Miss Jane Austen to Miss Austen

Steventon, 24 December 1798

My dearest Cassandra,

Thank you for your Christmas wishes. I return them a hundred-fold and would consider the new year prosperous if it proved rich in your presence. The Children's Ball went off famously. Anna adored the dancing and, in the spirit of entertaining the young people, I stood up twice with Alethea's brother, Harris. We may no longer call him 'little' as at seventeen he towers over us all, including James. Alas, his capacity for conversation remains stunted. I do not believe he uttered two words to me the whole half-hour.

To my delight, Mrs Chute was more willing to reveal all, from her naked shoulders to her suspicion that her husband was and remains in love with Lady Isabella. It seems old Mr Chute was not heartbroken as we had presumed by the disappearance of his first wife, owing to his preference for the hen over the chick. I doubt this alone would give him motive for murder, but, if Mary Ellen witnessed an indiscretion between her mother and her bridegroom on her wedding day, it might explain why she was so keen to escape the arrangement. Or, more darkly, it might have given the star-crossed lovers reason to hasten her departure from the wedding breakfast, and this realm altogether. Poor girl, was there no one she could confide in? If only Cecilia or Augusta could speak on her behalf. I'm sure either would know her heart.

Yours ever,
J.A.

PS Spoil the children for me and tell them, no matter what their mamma and pappa say, all their presents are really from Aunt Jane.

Miss Austen
Edward Austen's Esqr
Godmersham Park
Faversham
Kent

LETTER 7

From Lieutenant Francis Austen to Miss Jane Austen

HMS London, *Mediterranean Sea, 20 November 1798*

Dear Jane,

I know you tasked Charles with your commission, but I've no doubt he will forget the particulars, so I purchased a pair of white silk stockings each for you and Cassandra at the earliest opportunity. You owe me the handsome sum of one pound and four shillings, but I will write off the debt in recognition of your upcoming birthday. Life aboard the London is tiresome. Rations are scarce and the fleas are plentiful. Ship fever, too, is rife. We've had to confine the sick below deck and yesterday I flogged a midshipman for fraternizing with the ship's cat, whose occupation brings her in close contact with the source of the disease.

Worst of all, in such a small vessel, we have little hope of action. Pray remind Father he promised to write to General Matthew regarding my promotion. I may not be with you this Christmas, but do not think you are excused from attempting my charade:

My first dispels the darksome gloom;
You love my next wherever you roam.

My whole with cheering ray from far,
Gives comfort to the wandering tar.

Yours fraternally,
Frank

ESUOHTHGIL SI REWSNA EHT SP

Miss J. Austen
Steventon
Overton
Hants

Chapter Seven

On Christmas Day, Mary deigns to rise from her bedchamber and join the family for dinner. Her constant remarks on the gentrified nature of Mrs Lloyd's table, compared to Mrs Austen's, have everyone wishing she had remained in bed. According to Mary, despite being an impoverished widow, Mrs Lloyd is yet to embrace the new fashion for turkey and serves only the tenderest cut of beef, alongside a plum pudding she has fed with copious amounts of brandy and for no less than six months. Jane can tell, from the fine lines etched around her mother's tight smile, that it takes all of her Christian forbearance to refrain from pointing out to Mary that Mrs Lloyd and her two slight daughters may well afford to dine on beef and brandy all year. The Austens, though, have had countless strapping boys, both sons and scholars, to nourish, as well as an endless line of parishioners who are wont to caterwaul carols at the rectory front door on Christmas Day. The enormous gobbler Mrs Austen had selected for their feast, before she knew she would be blessed with

Mary and James's company, may not be the tenderest piece of meat, but it will ensure no one goes hungry.

Jane remains anxious to quiz her father on his double role in Mary Ellen's demise but, for the sake of family harmony, is also attempting to bridle her tongue at least until St Stephen's Day. It is not an easy task, especially as Rosalee is taking so long to serve the meal, and in the meantime is proving extremely generous with Mr Austen's claret wine.

'Who was it this time?' asks Mrs Austen, as her husband resumes his place at the head of the dining table in the best parlour. As usual, Jane's father spent Christmas morning delighting his parishioners with a short sermon and a long list of those who were to receive Christmas boxes. It is traditional for the poor to call at the rectory for sustenance on Christmas Day, but Mr Austen prefers to anticipate demand by distributing charity directly after the service in hopes his own family may be allowed to dine in peace. However, there are always some members of his congregation who, despite being absent from church, feel entitled to share in his dinner.

'Dame Kew, come to beg some meat and corn for her children. I already gave her husband a box, but I expect he's exchanged it for a jug of ale.'

'If you want to provide for the children, you must give to the mother not the father,' says Mrs Austen, articulating succinctly what generations of lawyers arguing for the bride's interest have struggled to define in lengthy and protracted marriage settlements.

'I know, but he was so peremptory in his request I could not refuse him.' He sighs, as Rosalee unceremoniously dumps a jug of butter sauce on the table, spilling grease on Mrs Austen's finest linen. The maid is red-cheeked and, Jane suspects, privately fuming at the additional guests. Mrs Austen refused to engage any help with the cooking, anticipating there would be only herself, her husband and Jane at table this year, and a simple tray would do for the three of them. Instead, Rosalee has singlehandedly cooked a full two-course dinner for five, not allowing for Anna, who will eat only potatoes, and Edward, who fusses in his crib beside his mother. Added to that, she, too, must listen politely as Mary pronounces judgement on every dish. The maid's eyes are bloodshot and her hands are shaking as she deposits the centrepiece of the meal, Jane's old nemesis the white turkey, before the family.

Mr Austen slumps at the sight of the enormous bird. 'Would you mind carving, James?'

'Of course, Father.' James, who has had his own sermon to deliver and parishioners to contend with, relishes the task and Jane, once again, is struck by the thought of how comfortable he looks acting the master of the rectory. After serving Mr and Mrs Austen, and his wife, he places a thin slice of breast on Jane's plate. 'Will that do?'

'Whatever portion Father deems appropriate,' Jane quips, despite herself.

Mr Austen narrows his eyes, the vertical lines cutting

deeper into his cheeks. 'What's that supposed to mean?'

'Nothing,' Jane replies, realizing she has been too tart in her reply. Her resolution to maintain peace did not last so long as the first course.

'Don't nothing me, my girl. I know your saucy tone when I hear it.'

It is no use, season of goodwill or not, she cannot contain her dissatisfaction with her father's behaviour towards Mary Ellen. 'What exactly was Ned referring to when he wrote "I gave my consent to the dissolution of the trust and advise Father to do likewise"?'

The table falls silent. Even Anna, sensing a shift in mood, desists from clattering her fork against her plate as Mr Austen leans back in his seat. 'He was merely alluding to some paperwork I undertook for one of our neighbours.'

'Which neighbour?'

'Must we, today of all days?' replies Mr Austen. Jane refuses to lower her gaze from her father's until he answers in full. 'Lady Isabella Portal's.'

'I suspected as much. You and Ned were signatories on the trust that excluded Mary Ellen from ever inheriting a portion of her mother's fortune, weren't you?'

'No . . .' Mr Austen splutters, feigning innocence. 'It was myself, Mr Chute and Mr Knight. Neddy simply inherited the responsibility. But why are you so angry with me? It was not my decision to disinherit Mary

Ellen. That was entirely her mother's doing. I simply acted as trustee as a favour to a neighbour.'

Jane cannot understand how her father, who usually gives every indication of being an enlightened, rational man, can be so contrary when it comes to his involvement in the fate of Mary Ellen. 'Your name is on the marriage certificate that sparked her downfall *and* on the settlement ensuring she could never recover from it. That makes you doubly complicit in my eyes.'

'Jane!' Mrs Austen cries. 'It is not for your father to decide how Lady Isabella dispenses her fortune.'

'No, but as a Christian he might have counselled her to show forgiveness towards her daughter. Or, failing that, refused to be party to such malice. Would you cut me out so, if I could not abide by your wishes for my future?'

Mr Austen's expression sours. 'No, Jane. Your mother and I might seek to guide you, but we have never once sought to impose. Indeed, I fear, from your manner of addressing me now, that we allow you too much liberty.'

Jane has gone too far. Her father indulges her curiosity and outspoken nature, but he will not stand for insolence from his children. 'Forgive me, Pappa. But did it not strike you as odd that she was so ready to throw off her daughter? Or that Mr Chute, Mary Ellen's own husband, was so willing to impoverish her?'

'Lady Isabella has a vindictive temper.' Mr Austen sighs, as if defeated by the vehemence of Lady Isabella's disposition, even now. 'Having made her acquaintance yourself, you must understand that?'

'I do . . . But to disinherit Mary Ellen so soon after she vanished. It's almost as if one or all of the parties involved in altering the settlement knew that she would never return to claim her share.'

'Jane! What are you accusing us of now? And in front of Anna!' says Mrs Austen, flushing pink as she belatedly realizes her granddaughter has left the table in favour of undressing and dressing her doll in her new Christmas fashions for the third time that day. 'Any more of this, and I'll think you believe *we* killed the poor girl and hid her body in the cellar.'

'Well, did you?' asks Jane. She can think of no obvious motive for her mother and father to murder Mary Ellen and conceal her corpse in their disused cellar but, in the interest of fairness, she supposes she should not automatically exclude them from her investigation. As her enquiry is met with horrified countenances, she can assume only that they are innocent. 'I'm sorry, that was unforgivable of me. But, supposing Mary Ellen had taken refuge in the cellar after fleeing her marriage and attempting to conceal herself from the search party, could she have become trapped?' If her family will not assist her in investigating a possible murder, she must at least garner their help in ruling out the possibility that Mary Ellen died by misadventure.

'No,' replies Mrs Austen. 'The ceiling is so low,

she could easily have pushed open the trapdoor and escaped through the kitchen.'

Jane recalls the panic in her throat as she realized the latch had fallen behind her and she was trapped in the pantry. 'Unless the pantry was locked from the outside?'

Mrs Austen shakes her head, dismissively. 'If that was the case, why would the remains be in the cellar rather than in the pantry?'

'Because the pantry is not wide enough to lie down to sleep in, but the cellar is? Or because something heavy was left on top of the trapdoor, preventing Mary Ellen from reaching it?'

'No, surely not.' Mrs Austen pales.

Given Jane's mother is the most likely person to have latched the pantry or placed a box on the trap-door inadvertently causing the slow, torturous death of anyone trapped in the cellar, Jane cannot blame her for being unwilling to countenance either possibility. She turns to her brother instead. 'James, is it possible to open the exterior hatch from inside the cellar?'

'I cannot say. I certainly took care not to let it close after me.' He spreads his arms and lays the backs of his hands on the table, in a gesture of appease-ment. 'But, Jane, we have no reason to believe the remains are Mary Ellen's. Mr Chute certainly did not think so.'

'He's viewed them already?' From James's rueful glance towards Mr Austen, Jane senses her father and brother had contrived to keep Mr Chute's undertaking a secret from her.

'He did, first thing this morning. He said he wanted to get the terrible business over with before calling on Lady Isabella. Really, Jane, it was badly done of you to expose him to such an ordeal. He could find no clue that the remains were Mary Ellen's. Instead he agreed with Mr Craven's verdict, that they are most probably those of a deceased soldier. The regimental coat is too difficult to ignore.'

But Jane refuses to be swayed by Mr Chute's testimony. The remains were so severely decomposed as to bear little resemblance to any person in life. It was Lady Isabella, rather than he, Jane had hoped might recognize something, a mother being so much more familiar with a daughter and her belongings than a husband of only a few hours. 'Unless it wasn't an accident, and the coat belonged to the perpetrator, rather than the victim of the crime?'

'Stop this at once,' cries James, as Anna returns, her doll now rather formally attired for a family dinner in a miniature version of Jane's robe à *la turque*. 'May I remind you we have no reason to suspect that the remains are Mary Ellen's. In fact, we have no reason at all to suspect Mary Ellen is dead.'

'Oh, she's most certainly dead,' says Mary. 'The living can't haunt the woods.'

James casts his eyes to the ceiling, exasperated at his wife's lack of support. 'That's just a ghost story,

Mary. No one really believes her spirit roams the woods.'

'Lady Isabella does. She claimed Mary Ellen was at the window, knocking to be let in, but her ladyship bade her daughter go away and declared she would never forgive her for humiliating her. This was after everyone thought the disease was sure to prove fatal, and even the apothecary had instructed her to prepare her soul for death.'

'That will have been the fever talking.' James sighs. 'I expect Lady Isabella was delirious.'

Mary takes a forkful of plum pudding, then spits it into her handkerchief as she considers. 'Mother did say the commotion occurred on Christmas Day, when Lady Isabella had reached the height of her illness. The next morning, her fever had broken, and against all expectations, she began to show signs of recovery. She credited Mamma for her salvation, of course. But, you know, when people are near to dying, they are often visited by the spirits of their dead relations seeking to guide them on their path to the afterlife.' She smiles, keen to impress her family's superior intimacy not only with Lady Isabella but also her dead daughter.

By now, Mrs Austen has met her limit. 'Will every-one please leave off speaking of ghosts and murder and enjoy their dinner? Rosalee has worked very hard to prepare this meal, and instead of showing your appreciation, you are all determined to bicker. Is that really how we should be celebrating the birth of Our Lord and Saviour?' she says, shaming the table into divine contemplation of the mountain of uneaten food before them.

Despite her mother's instructions, Jane can only push the food across her plate. Her appetite disappeared with her temerity to question her father. Mercifully, she is spared from forcing herself to eat by a loud knock. 'I'll go,' she says, thankful for the chance to escape and mindful that Rosalee, who has finished serving, will be taking the opportunity to eat. But when Jane passes through the kitchen, grabbing a few freshly baked mince pies and wrapping them in cloth, she finds Rosalee helping herself to the dregs of the claret. In the spirit of Christmas, Jane pretends not to have witnessed the maid's indiscretion, or to have heard her hiccup, and proceeds directly to the front door.

Chapter Eight

J ane opens the door to find two elderly women, whom she just about recognizes, beneath coarse woollen cloaks and multiple layers of knitted scarves, as Dame Hutchins and Dame Staples. Both attend her father's church occasionally and are more regular recipients of his charity. She waits patiently as they utter a dismal ditty, which may or may not be a traditional Christmas carol. Jane cannot tell as she is not familiar with the words or melody, and neither, it seems, are they. Instead, the women mouth gibberish or hum unharmoniously each time they reach a new verse. As they complete a fifth round of the chorus, Jane foists the mince pies on the nearest. 'Compliments of the season!' she says, hoping her gift will bring the performance to a close. Alas, from the way the pair continue to linger, nudging each other with their elbows, it is clear they were hoping for more. 'I'm sorry but my father has already given away all his ale. There is plenty of dinner, if you'd like to come inside and take a plate?'

After some vicious prodding, Dame Hutchins accepts her role as spokeswoman. 'Is it true the skeleton young Mr Austen found at Deane belonged to Miss Portal? Only if it is she we'd like to know where she is to be buried so that we may pay our respects.'

Jane is taken aback. From Lady Isabella's account of her daughter's short life, she did not expect Mary Ellen would be known, much less held in esteem, among the villagers. 'Where did you hear that?'

'Rosa –' begins Dame Staples, before Dame Hutchins can cut her off.

'It's no matter where we heard it. Is it true?'

Jane steps out into the lane and pulls the door to behind her, heedless of the bitter wind blowing through the cambric of her morning dress. It would not do to upset the peace further by incurring Mary's wrath for allowing a draught to billow through the rectory in the direction of Edward, or inviting more of her father's censure for interrogating his parishioners. 'Were you acquainted with Miss Portal?'

'We saw her from time to time, miss.' Dame Hutchins lowers the hood of her red cloak. 'We both served as milkmaids at Ashe, in our younger days.'

'That's why we've such beauteous complexions.' Dame Staples cackles. Despite their advanced ages, and deep-set wrinkles, their countenances remain unmarred by the pox.

'Can you tell me a little about her?' asks Jane. As Lady Isabella refuses, and Mr Chute has failed, to identify the skeleton, she is running out of people to speak to who may be able to help establish a link between Mary Ellen and the remains.

'Why, she was most amiable.' Dame Hutchins smiles softly, the question clearly evoking a tender memory. 'Never too proud to do her duty, even if she was the granddaughter of an earl. And so patient towards her sisters. From the moment they could walk, she would lead them around the farm, showing them the animals and pointing out all the hazards they must be careful to avoid.'

'Generous to a fault, too.' Dame Staples nods heartily. 'It was a rare day I left the farm without a half-dozen eggs or a pat of butter. I fear she knew Mr Stevens, God rest his soul, did not allow me to keep my earnings, and she always said she would not have my children go hungry while I was employed at Ashe.'

'There were those who would try to take advantage of her good nature,' adds Dame Hutchins. 'But she was no milksop, mind. Miss Portal could always tell if one of the workers, or even the animals, was trying to get the better of her. If she wasn't in the dairy, she'd be in the stables, schooling the flightiest ponies.'

Jane's heart sinks. How sad that such a spirited character could have been broken by her mother's demands. 'If truth be told, I have no proof the skeleton was Miss Portal's. The magistrate certainly thinks not, but I cannot help wondering if it might be her. It seems too much of a coincidence otherwise. Unless you can tell me of some other woman or boy who disappeared around the same time as her?'

'None at all, miss.' Dame Hutchins frowns, seeming to consider this quandary. 'But if there's even a chance it's Miss Portal, she should be laid to rest at St Nicholas's with Miss Cecilia and Miss Augusta. It's what she would have wanted.'

Jane nods her agreement. Thankfully, the frost has not abated, but it cannot last for ever, which means Jane is running out of time to save the deceased from being buried unnamed in a common grave. 'Did you ever see Miss Portal, after the morning of her wedding?'

'Not hide nor hair, miss,' replies Dame Hutchins

'And was there any talk among the farm men about where she might have been going when she left her father's house?'

'Oh, plenty of talk . . .'

'Yes?' Jane's heart lifts with the desperate hope that the women may know something Mary Ellen's mother and husband did not.

'That she was living in a hollow tree, trapping her dinner.' Dame Staples laughs. 'Or that she had lost her heart to a soldier and gone to follow the drum!'

'Could either of those have been the case, do you think?'

Dame Hutchins eyes fill with pity that Jane could be so naïve as to believe such idle talk. 'Miss Portal was too sensible a girl to lose her head over a redcoat, and she was far too proud to go poaching. Besides, she so rarely left the estate that I can't see how she'd have run into a soldier and, as clever as she was, I never saw her with a snare. I really can't think where she'd have run to, for she seemed to lead a sheltered life, even for a young lady.'

'What about her ghost?' Jane asks, remembering Mary's assurances that Mary Ellen's spirit lingers in the neighbourhood. 'Have you ever seen that?'

'Her ghost?' Even Dame Staples stares at her quizzically.

'It's meant to haunt the woods between Steventon and Deane.'

'That's just an old story meant to keep children from wandering off on their own,' explains Dame Hutchins.

'Of course.' Jane laughs, feeling foolish for raising the possibility. But for all their candour, the women have provided no more insight as to Mary Ellen's intentions than Lady Isabella or Mr Chute. Can Mary Ellen really have been kept so isolated? 'Did she have any other friends or acquaintances hereabouts that you know of? Anyone at all that she spoke to?'

The pair exchange a furtive glance, as if revealing any alliances to Jane might entail betraying Mary Ellen. Finally, Dame Staples breaks her silence. 'She and Mrs Terry, that was Miss Bolton, were great friends.'

'Mrs Terry? And is she any relation to Mr Bolton of Ashe Farm?' As the Terrys are the Austens' neighbours, Jane is familiar with the family, but she was not aware of any connection between Mrs Terry and Lady Isabella's tenant.

'She's his daughter, miss,' Dame Hutchins explains, and shoots her companion a reproving glare. Despite coming to her for information, Dame Hutchins is not especially eager to share all she knows with Jane. 'Mr Bolton was Sir Robert's steward. After the baronet died, he took on the lease for the farm. But none of us would work for that old miser – he'd take a measuring stick to the cream and accuse you of skimming it before he'd pay you an honest day's wage.'

'I see. Well, thank you, you've been most helpful. I shall visit Mrs Terry, and I promise I shall let you know where the remains are to be buried.'

'Please do, miss. God bless you for remembering poor Miss Portal, and a merry Christmas to you.'

'And to you.' Jane pats Dame Staples's arm. As she does, the scratchy texture of her cloak invokes a memory. Two different types of red wool were wrapped around the mummified head: the finer scarlet of an officer's coat and something more closely akin to this duller, rougher cloth. 'Wait! If you don't mind my asking, where did you purchase your cloak?'

Dame Staples turns, confusion clouding her eyes. 'My cloak?'

'Yes. Pray tell me, where did you get it?'

She colours. 'Why, the poorhouse, miss. They give them freely to all who are obliged to remain there.'

'Oh . . . Well, it looks very warm, and the shade is decidedly cheerful,' Jane replies, ashamed to have embarrassed her. '*Coquelicot*, as the French call it. I believe it is to be all the fashion this winter.'

The women shuffle off down the lane, exchanging confused countenances, which imply that Jane has run completely mad and probably should not therefore be trusted as to her suspicions regarding the identity of the remains found at Deane. Jane, too, cannot help wondering if she might have been wrong. Mary Ellen would hardly have been likely to own a cloak from the poorhouse. Unless she died while attempting to return to her family after a miserable time trying to survive on her own. But that would not explain why she was still wearing the white silk. Perhaps she was killed soon after fleeing by two persons acting together, an officer and a woman who had visited the poorhouse. Yet how strange that both perpetrators would have left their clothing with the victim, especially in the depths of winter. It is yet one more piece of this morbid puzzle that Jane cannot fathom.

Chapter Nine

A flurry of snow, not so dense as to dissuade James from his plans to ride with the hunt, but heavy enough to bleach the rolling hills and prevent Jane from walking out, marks the arrival of St Stephen's Day. Mrs Austen and Mary continue to disagree on everything, from the likelihood of the French returning to unite the Irish against King George to the correct manner in which to swaddle Edward, while Mr Austen retreats to his library, weary of dissent in his ranks. Despite her apology, Jane's father remains out of sorts. It is not often, if ever, that they argue and she regrets the breach between them.

To distract herself, she composes nonsense about a particularly despotic queendom of fairies and acts out their antics with the help of Anna's doll, much to the delight of the little girl. The tense household is a far cry from the Christmases of Jane's youth, when the rectory was crowded with young people and James would press his advantage as eldest to corral the restless band of relations and schoolboys into performing a theatrical composition of his choice. Jane was considered too young to be granted a part and, instead, spent the season watching from the makeshift wings in the family barn, studying the bewitching performances of her elder cousins, Eliza and Jane Cooper. With each year that passes, she finds herself growing more and more nostalgic for those rowdy Christmases, fuelled by the sanctioned transgressions of mistletoe and theatre.

She supposes she must reconcile herself to a more retired way of living. With Bonaparte's ambition having disrupted the Continent, and the war having spilled so far as Egypt, Henry, Frank and Charles are unlikely to return to Hampshire in the foreseeable future. Even if they were to be granted leave, she doubts those fine young men would stand for James dressing them up as barbaric sultans or saucy servants. In any case, since his ordination, James has turned his pen away from theatrical prologues and towards pious sermons. In her bleaker moments, Jane fears even Cassandra might be persuaded to remain in Kent by the offer of some eligible gentleman. Neither Mrs Austen nor Neddy's wife, Elizabeth, was gauche enough to express their reasons for prevailing on her to extend her visit to Godmersham but, Jane knows, they are united in their scheme to throw her beautiful, sweet-tempered sister in the way of as many rich men as possible.

At last, on 28 December, Jane wakes to a brilliant blue sky, which promises to hold long enough for her to call on Mary Ellen's only known confidante, Mrs

Terry. The Terrys' farm lies a few miles to the west of Steventon along the road to Basingstoke. After being confined for several days, Jane delights in crunching over the still-frozen ground, her pattens slicing through icy puddles. The Terrys' fields envelop her father's glebe lands and, as Mr Austen is keen to maintain warm relations with all of his neighbours, but especially those who have the good manners to pay their tithes, Jane has been a regular visitor to the farm since she was old enough to accompany her father in the saddle. No matter the season, Mr Terry is always delighted to be distinguished by the rector's company and pauses in his work to apologize for the humble nature of his abode and the uncouthness of his manner. All this, despite it being evident from the handsome brick and timber farmhouse, and the herd of plump Alderney cows huddled together in the pasture, that the Terrys are far wealthier than the Austens and not in the least uncivilized.

Relations between the two men are so cordial that Jane might have persuaded her father to call on his neighbour today, thereby providing herself with a convenient excuse for imposing on his wife. However, since Mr Austen remains unequivocal in his admonishment of Jane's investigation, she resolves to complete her mission alone. Her heart smarts at being unable to confide in him. She has always known her father to be a sympathetic man, and it perplexes her that he can accept no culpability in Mary Ellen's downfall. Instead,

Jane resorts to the feeble excuse of delivering a book to Miss Terry, the family's eldest daughter. Since Miss Terry has never shown the slightest interest in any of Jane's books, and Jane is loath to surrender any to one who does not take pleasure in reading, she has taken great care in selecting the volume tucked into her basket.

'Miss Jane.' Mrs Terry opens the door looking more flustered than Jane, who has walked nearly a mile out of her way and climbed three stiles in her attempt to avoid passing directly by Mr Terry's bull. 'What a pleasant surprise. I feared you might be Mrs Lefroy, come to pester Mr Terry about the cowpox again. And after he was so brutish the last time she was here. But please don't say my girls were expecting you? They set off for Basingstoke half an hour ago with Miss Bigg in her carriage. Oh, how rude! I can only offer my apologies on their behalf, for it must have slipped their minds.'

Jane, who had hidden in the hedgerow as Alethea's phaeton, packed with female Terrys, passed her on the main road, does her best to affect disappointment. 'Oh dear. I'm so sorry to have missed them. But it is my own fault, for I did not give notice of my visit. The day was so clear and bright, I thought some exercise would benefit my constitution. And I wanted to deliver Miss Terry this book, which, at our last meeting, she expressed a particular interest in reading.'

'She did?' Mrs Terry glances doubtfully at Volume One of *Fordyce's Sermons*, nestled in Jane's basket.

'Very much so.' Jane has left Volume Two at home, in case she needed to return and interview Mrs Terry further – and because weight is pressing on her conscience for inflicting such drivel on Miss Terry. God forbid her mother believes it an honour that the rector's daughter is making efforts to improve her mind and forces her to read it.

'How kind you are.' Mrs Terry removes her apron, wiping her floury hands on the fabric and handing it to her elderly maid, before reluctantly accepting the book. 'Won't you take some tea before returning to Steventon? You must be half frozen, and we have a good fire going.'

Jane smiles sweetly. The Terrys' impeccable hospitality is one thing she can always rely on. 'If you're certain I would be no imposition?'

'Not at all.' Mrs Terry throws the door wide and practically drags Jane over the threshold. Once inside, it is clear Jane is very much an imposition. The faint, beer-like scent of yeast permeates the air, suggesting she has disturbed baking day, and the various little Terrys call their mother from the door frame to continue with her telling of Mother Goose. Regardless, the unrelentingly civil Mrs Terry abandons her bread to sink and chases her younger children back to their nursery, before politely asking her maid to bring a tray to the best parlour. The snug room, overlooking an ornamental garden, is comfortably rather than elegantly furnished. With the additional charm of colourful paper chains pinned to the low beams and boughs of bay, holly, yew and fir adorning every ledge and windowsill, it is even more welcoming than usual. Mrs Terry begs Jane to take the Windsor chair nearest the inglenook fireplace, while she draws a stool and perches beside her. On any other day, Jane would assure Mrs Terry her children were no bother and insist on reading to them in the kitchen as she finished her kneading. This morning, however, Jane is most grateful for her hostess's full attention.

After she has made brusque but necessary enquiries as to the health of all the Terrys, and rattled off a brief account as to the whereabouts and minor ailments of all her near relations, Jane comes to the true purpose of her visit. 'I wonder, Mrs Terry, if you heard about the skeleton my brother uncovered in the cellar at Deane Parsonage?'

As anticipated, Mrs Terry nods eagerly. Mrs Lefroy was right: the only thing that spreads faster than disease is gossip. 'A soldier, they say. Fallen on hard times and frozen to death, God rest his soul. If only he'd called here, Mr Terry would have seen him right for it would not be Christian to refuse charity to one who has served King and country.'

'Yes, well . . . I know the magistrate declared the deceased a soldier, due to the corpse being wrapped in a regimental jacket. But, having had the chance to examine it briefly myself, I wondered if it might be the remains of the missing Miss Portal.'

'Oh . . . oh . . .' Mrs Terry's voice wavers and her

teacup rattles in its dish as she places it on the tray between them. 'Mary Ellen? Could it really be her, after all this time?'

At her obvious distress, unexpected tears prick Jane's eyes. Mrs Terry is more affected by the possible dire fate of Mary Ellen than the young lady's husband or, indeed, her own mother. At last, Jane has found someone who truly cared for her. 'Please don't mistake me, Mrs Terry. I have no conclusive proof.' For the first time since she began her investigation, Jane experiences a twinge of guilt at implying the remains may be those of Mary Ellen. It would be most cruel of her to raise expectations of solving the mystery among Mary Ellen's loved ones if she cannot find evidence that the remains are hers, or to distress them unnecessarily at the prospect of the young lady meeting such a miserable death if she is still alive. 'It's just that the remains were so diminutive in stature, I earnestly believe they could only have been those of a woman or a boy. And they had been there for some time, possibly for as long as sixteen years, and we know the parsonage was empty at the time Mary Ellen disappeared.'

Mrs Terry clutches a hand to her breast. 'But I don't understand. *Why* would Mary Ellen be in the cellar at Deane?'

'I was hoping you might be able to help me understand that.'

'Me?'

'You were friends, I believe?'

'It's true that we grew up alongside each other . . .' Mrs Terry squeezes her eyes shut and swallows hard, all thoughts of ruined loaves and neglected children cast aside. 'My father began in this county as steward for Sir Robert. I was an only child, and lonelier than ever after my mother passed away. We lived in a small cottage on the edge of the estate and, from the age of about nine, he began to take me with him while he worked. There was no one to object as Lady Isabella and Sir Robert lived almost entirely in Town and all three girls were left to the servants to manage. Some of my fondest recollections are of exploring the park with Mary Ellen and the younger girls, Cecilia and Augusta, but it was Mary Ellen I was closest to in age and temperament. We may have been of very different stations, but nothing came between us. That was until Mary Ellen reached marriageable age, and her mother decided to take notice of her.' There is an edge to Mrs Terry's voice when she mentions Lady Isabella. 'They never got on, you know.'

'They were very different, by all accounts.'

'Yes, and yet in many ways alike.' Mrs Terry laughs, mirthlessly. 'Both as bull-headed and rash as they were beautiful. You wouldn't know that now, of course. Lady Isabella was horribly disfigured by her illness, and I don't believe she kept so much as a single portrait of Mary Ellen. I wish I had cut a lock of her hair, or had something else to remember her by, but all I have is my memories.'

Jane settles into the chair, relieved to have found

someone who can attest to Mary Ellen's true character. She has been a shadow, a wisp of a girl blotted out by her cruel parents. Only now, under Mrs Terry's description, is Jane beginning to get a sense of who she really was. 'Can you describe her to me? Her appearance, I mean.'

'Mary Ellen? Why, she was a beauty. Long raven hair, and eyes the most peculiar shade of blue, almost violet. Given a few years, she would have been even more striking than her mother.'

Perhaps part of Lady Isabella's rationale for affiancing her daughter to an antisocial country squire was in fear she would eclipse her mother in fashionable circles. Regardless, the description does not help, as Jane can remember no eyes in the mummified head and, although there were a few strands of long, dark hair, they may have become discoloured after death. 'And in stature?'

'Oh, she was very well formed. A few inches shorter than yourself, and plumper, more like your sister.'

Jane suppresses a smile. Mrs Terry is hinting that Mary Ellen possessed the sort of figure that men are apt to admire. The description of her height is all Jane needs to know that the skeleton could be Mary Ellen's, despite Mr Chute attesting otherwise. 'And did she ever confide in you about her objections to her marriage – or her plans to run away?'

'Never,' says Mrs Terry, her expression becoming pained. 'For I did not speak to her once after her engagement was announced. I was married myself by then, with my eldest daughter in my arms and another on the way. Still, Mary Ellen would sometimes visit me, here at the farmhouse. But, from the moment Sir Robert announced the engagement, all communication between us ceased. I begged my father to carry a message to her, but he would not risk his position and said I was foolish to ask. He had long warned me there would be a day when I'd need to forget our girlhood fondness for one another. For, as he put it, a Mrs Chute can hardly call on a Mrs Terry.' She chokes on the words. Despite the years, the enforced separation remains raw. 'I even persuaded Mr Terry to drive me to the park once, so that I might deliver a note myself, but the housekeeper told me that Mary Ellen was in disgrace and not allowed any letters. Especially from myself, for Lady Isabella did not approve of our friendship.'

Jane muses. How odd that if Mary Ellen had a friend as devoted as Mrs Terry she would not think to go to *her* upon fleeing her marriage. She could have been on her way to the farmhouse when she was killed, of course, but Deane is slightly too far north to lie directly in the path between Ashe Park and the Terrys' farm. 'Can you remember the last time you saw her?'

Mrs Terry takes a handkerchief from her pocket and dabs her eyes. 'I stood outside your father's church to see her wed but I don't know if she saw me.'

Jane's heart constricts at the pitiful image of Mrs

Terry waiting for a glimpse of Mary Ellen in her wedding clothes, hoping that a glance between them might convey all that had been lost. She seems to have loved her more than anyone else Jane has spoken to. 'Do you think Mary Ellen might have attempted to catch the stagecoach from Deane Gate Inn?'

'Perhaps . . .' Mrs Terry blinks, as if this thought has only just occurred to her. 'She did take it once, from Town. It was only a few months before she went missing, after my father was sent to collect her from school.'

'She went away to school?' Jane asks. Everyone has assured her Mary Ellen had no life outside Ashe Park, but if she was educated, she may have formed attachments entirely unknown to her family and neighbours.

But Mrs Terry shakes her head dismissively. 'Only for a couple of weeks. Her mother insisted. Looking back, I expect it was in preparation for marrying her off to a wealthy husband, but it was too late. Mary Ellen's character was already formed. She had no interest in painting screens or speaking French, or whatever it is you young ladies learn to do at such places,' Mrs Terry says, as Jane smiles. While the first school she and Cassandra had attended brought only disaster, the second, Madame La Tournelle's establishment in Reading, was a far more enjoyable experience. She doubts either was comparable to whatever prestigious seminary Lady Isabella dispatched Mary Ellen to, yet she probably learned as much. 'She told me afterwards what a humiliation it was to be forced to attend at such an age. She made it her objective to be so troublesome that the school mistress would dismiss her. When that didn't work, she tried to escape, and then she really was expelled!'

'She had tried to flee before, then?'

'Yes.' Mrs Terry laughs through her tears. 'The school mistress discovered her half out of the window!'

'And do you know where she was going, if she had been successful?'

'Why, back to the park. Where else would she have gone? She was as pleased as Punch when my father arrived to fetch her. I expect it was meant as a punishment, to be forced to ride with a servant rather than be granted the use of the family carriage, but they got along famously. He could not be severe with her, for he had ever held a soft spot for Mary Ellen and her sisters. She laughed all the way, telling him how satisfied she was in achieving her aim without having to risk her neck in dropping from the window.'

'But if she despised her mother and father so, why would she wish to return to Ashe?'

'You forget, Lady Isabella and Sir Robert were so rarely at home. And Cecilia and Augusta were there.'

'Oh . . .' Jane hesitates. She had been only seven when she willingly sacrificed the safety and comfort of home to be with her sister. She does not doubt Mary Ellen would abandon her education, as well as all decorum, to be reunited with hers. 'And so, when she finally managed to run away, was it because there was someone else she hoped to marry? One of the officers from the Buckinghamshire regiment, perhaps? I believe they were passing through Hampshire at the time.'

Mrs Terry scoffs at the idea. 'She wasn't the sort to be taken in by a redcoat, however handsome. She would have objected to the match with Mr Chute because she never wanted to marry at all, let alone someone her mother had chosen for her. Oh, everything would have been so much easier if she had been born a man. We so often talked of it, how different things would be if only she could inherit her father's estate.'

'Another thing I cannot fathom is how nobody saw her leave. Do you think she might have borrowed a garment belonging to one of the servants at the park to disguise herself? Something like a rough red woollen cloak, the type those thrown upon the parish are provided with?'

'Oh, no, not Mary Ellen.' Mrs Terry wrinkles her nose. 'She could be as vain as her mother when it came to finery. Even when carrying out her duties on the farm, she'd always be very smartly dressed.'

'Her *duties*?' When Dame Hutchins said that she and the other dairy maids saw Mary Ellen from time to time, Jane had assumed it was in the dignified manner in which she sometimes greets her father's labourers. She had not expected Mary Ellen would take on any share of the work.

'She managed the dairy. I know you young ladies are above such occupations now, but there was a time when it was considered a great accomplishment. Even the grandest of ladies took an interest in husbandry,' Mrs Terry explains, as Jane considers her mother's preoccupation with her poultry yard. 'Cecilia took it on afterwards. It's not like now, when all you girls want to do is put on airs and read nonsense.' She casts a disparaging look at *Fordyce's Sermons*. Jane is beginning to wish she had chosen a less ridiculous title. 'To think, Mary Ellen may have been there, just a few miles away in Deane, all this time when I have searched for her everywhere.'

'You have?' Jane is buoyed to know she has not been alone in investigating Mary Ellen's strange disappearance. Without her sisters to mourn her, a cruel mother and an indifferent husband of only a few hours, she had feared the memory of her short life had become nothing more than a haunting tale to frighten children.

'Wherever I have travelled since she disappeared, I have searched for Mary Ellen's face in the crowd. Every time I visit the marketplace at Basingstoke or Winchester, I cannot help but seek to catch a glimpse of her. A few years after we were married, Mr Terry and I journeyed so far as to the island,' she says, referring, Jane supposes, to the Isle of Wight. 'Every time we stepped into a fresh inn, or passed through a new village in the coach, I would cast my eyes around for her, but she was never there.' Mrs Terry lets out an anguished sigh. 'And all this time, she may have been in the cellar of the parsonage. Would she have gone in there to seek shelter, then perished from the cold, do you think?'

'That's certainly what Mr Craven believes happened to whoever it is.'

Mrs Terry shakes her head. 'But Mary Ellen was more than capable of building a fire. And why hide in the cellar, if the parsonage was empty?'

'Perhaps she was hiding from the search party.'

'You mentioned a soldier's coat. Why would she have that?'

'I . . . I don't know.' Jane cannot bring herself to add to Mrs Terry's pain by voicing her fear that, if the garment did not belong to the corpse, it may have belonged to whoever put it there.

By the sudden look of anguish on Mrs Terry's features, she seems to have come to her own terrible conclusion. 'I have tried to keep the hope in my breast that one day I might see her again . . .' she sobs, '. . . but in my heart, I knew she was dead. That something dreadful must have befallen her almost immediately after she went missing.'

'How?' Jane may be led by her own intuition, but she cannot help questioning the veracity of it in others.

'Because she never came back.'

'To challenge the alterations her mother made to her settlement?'

'To nurse her sisters, after they became sick.' Mrs Terry gazes at her openly, as if this much should have been obvious. 'She may have been at war with Lady Isabella, but she adored Cecilia and Augusta. She was more of a mother to them than her own mother was.'

From Jane's impressions of Lady Isabella, she can well believe this. 'You will remember the outbreak?'

'Not with any great clarity, I'm afraid. I was only a child, and in ill-health myself at the time.' Jane's enduring memory of the winter of 1783 is being confined to the rectory and scolded to wrap up very warm about the throat whenever she was allowed into the garden for air. Only now is she beginning to understand why her mother was so determined to keep all her children at home while sickness raged throughout the county.

'Sir Robert brought back the disease from Town. His pustules were already weeping by the time he reached the park. If he'd had any care for his family, he would have stayed away. After that, the infection spread like a flame. Anyone with any self-preservation abandoned their post immediately. One by one, all who remained were struck down, family and servants alike, until there was no one to care for the sick. My father was one of the first to enter the house after Lady Isabella recovered and demanded his assistance. He told me he found Cecilia and Augusta in bed, side by side, hands clutched for comfort and their faces covered with a sheet – while the rest of the dead were slumped in corners, flies hovering about their eyes and mouths. How Lady Isabella survived, I do not know.'

'But I thought those who had already had the disease were called in to care for them?' says Jane, remembering Mary's claims that her mother had nursed Lady Isabella.

'At first, yes. But soon the situation became so grave, and it was clear there was nothing that could be done for the household. No one would set foot in the place. I would have gone, but Mr Terry forbade me.'

'You would have risked your life to care for Cecilia and Augusta?' From Mrs Terry's smooth complexion, Jane is confident she cannot be immune.

'They were like sisters to me. And I would have risked nothing, for I had already had the cowpox, and therefore would not have contracted the disease.' She holds her hands to the firelight, and Jane can just about make out small silver patches on the backs of each.

'You believe the substance of Dr Jenner's *Inquiry*, then?'

'Oh, Miss Jane, when one grows up on a dairy farm, as I did, one does not need a doctor to explain the benefits of the cowpox. But my assurances were not enough for Mr Terry. He locked me in our bedroom and nailed a plank to the window! Mary Ellen would not have stood for such treatment. If she had been alive, she'd have found her way back to the park. I would not wish her dead . . . but if those *are* her remains, I do hope you can prove so, and that she may be laid to rest beside her sisters.'

'As do I,' Jane muses.

Perhaps if Jane cannot find a way to prove that the remains are Mary Ellen's, or even persuade Mr Craven that whoever they belonged to was killed unlawfully, she may go some way to satisfying her conscience by persuading her father to inter them at Steventon. Mr Austen may not approve of Jane inserting herself into the magistrate's investigation, but he is not averse to turning a blind eye to ecclesiastical rules in the name of compassion. It could do no harm to offer an unidentified soul eternal sanctuary beneath the flagstones of St Nicholas's church, and she expects James would be pleased to be relieved of the responsibility. Then, at least, if Jane is right and the skeleton is Mary Ellen's, all three sisters would be reunited.

Chapter Ten

When Jane returns to the rectory, half frozen in person but her spirit warmed by Mrs Terry's constancy towards her friend, she alights upon a scene of domestic industry to rival that of any enterprising cottager. Her mother and Mary are so engrossed in their work that they have neglected to notice the sky has faded to a violet gloom and Rosalee really should have lit the candles. Rather than draw attention to the maid's failure, Jane holds a taper to the crackling fire and proceeds to light the room before greeting her family. Anna is arranging her dolls in the manner of a country dance, while Edward, fast asleep in his cradle, emits a series of quiet snores. Jane wants to kiss the baby's downy head, but Anna protested so much to her icy nose that she dare not disturb him too.

Finally, roused by the glow, Mrs Austen holds an infant's gown away from herself. 'We're making the preparations for Edward's christening.' She squints at the exquisite whitework embroidery she has so carefully stitched onto the bodice, much to the detriment of her ageing eyes. 'It is to be held at St Nicholas's on the first of January, and Mary will be churched on the same day. Afterwards, she and James will return to the parsonage.' From her mother's satisfied smile, Jane can tell Mrs Austen is anticipating the removal of her daughter-in-law with as much joy as she is looking forward to marking her grandson's entrance to the church. It is always gratifying to receive one's relations for Christmas, if only the better to appreciate their eventual removal. 'We shall toast a new life *and* a new year. Where, I might ask, have you been?'

'Visiting our neighbours. Mrs Terry sends her regards.' Jane sits on the arm of her father's usual chair, which, despite his increasingly unsubtle hints, Mary continues to occupy. 'Did you know she and Mary Ellen were bosom friends?'

Mrs Austen drops the gown into her lap. 'You're not still pursuing the idea that the remains are Mary Ellen's, are you? Your father was very clear in his command.'

'Yes, he was.' Jane smiles. 'Father bade me not to insert myself into the magistrate's investigation, and I can faithfully declare that I have not approached Mr Craven once on the topic.'

'Jane! You understood full well he meant for you to refrain from investigating altogether.'

'I'm sure Uncle Richard wouldn't mind.' Mary looks up from tying off a tiny rosebud along the rim of a baby's bonnet. 'He came to quite enjoy your questions the last time there was a murder in the neighbourhood.'

'All the more reason for me to obey my father.' Jane shudders. Mr Craven did come to appreciate her assistance when investigating the death of a young woman found bludgeoned to death at Deane House a few Christmases ago. In fact, he paid several visits to the rectory to compliment Jane on the clarity of her understanding afterwards. On the last occasion, he was so bold as to present her with a bouquet of daffodils cut from Mrs Lloyd's garden. Jane had to affect several violent sneezes to get him to take them away with him. She would rather not encourage such attentions from Mary's uncle. 'Does either of you know where the remains are now?'

'Austen promises that every last piece has been removed from the cellar and taken away to prepare for burial. I should not have agreed to return to the parsonage otherwise.'

'Prepared by whom?' asks Jane.

'That's hardly any of your concern,' replies Mrs Austen, a heavy note of caution in her voice.

With the tiniest amount of prodding, Jane is confident she could induce Mary to reveal the identity of whoever the corpse has been entrusted to, despite her family's collusion to keep from her all information pertaining to the matter. However, on reflection, Jane finds she does not need to apply to them for the answer to this mystery. There is only one person hereabouts who is trusted to 'prepare' the dead for their final journey. And the fact that her son, Jack Smith, was tasked with retrieving the remains from Deane lends weight to Jane's suspicion. She resolves to visit her former nurse, Dame Culham, first thing in the morning. 'But you're certain they have not been buried yet?'

Mrs Austen shakes her head wearily. 'No, the ground is still too hard to dig. And, given the deceased is already so decomposed as to be inoffensive, your father says there's no hurry.'

Jane nods, satisfied she still has time to convince her father to inter the remains at Steventon. It is not justice for Mary Ellen, but it might bring her spirit peace. 'Mrs Terry told me it was very hard to find anyone willing to visit the sick at Ashe Park. Did your mother tell you any more about what she saw or heard there?'

'No.'

'I suppose it was too awful to speak of.'

'No. Mother did not go to Ashe Park. Lady Isabella came to us.'

'Lady Isabella resided at Deane Parsonage throughout her illness?'

Mary harrumphs in irritation. Having been distracted by Jane's question, she has pulled her needle so far as to lose her thread. She takes the cotton between her lips then twists it to a sharp point, jabbing it towards the eye. 'My mother is not a nurse for hire, Jane. She took in Lady Isabella in deference to her position, and because she would not be turned away.'

Jane recalls Mrs Terry's words: *Anyone with any self-preservation abandoned their post immediately*. She had not anticipated this would include Lady Isabella. 'She fled the park, leaving her husband and two daughters to die?'

Unable to rethread her needle, Mary casts aside the bonnet. 'You don't understand, Jane. You've never been party to an outbreak, and you must pray to God you never are. If you think my scars are the worst of it, you've no idea. Once the wretched disease takes hold, every part of the body, inside and out, is covered in blisters so raw that it hurts to breathe. The pain is so great that the sufferer longs for death.' She pauses, and Jane is forced to look away in shame. She is not always as kind to Mary as she should be, but she does care for her greatly. 'When it was clear she could do no more than pray for her husband and daughters, Lady Isabella persuaded her steward to bring her to us, as her nearest neighbours – and, I suppose, because she knew we had already been afflicted so, and thus were more likely to give her quarter. She demanded my father convey her to her address in Town, but my mother knew we could not let her go. Even without a single pustule present on her person, she could tell Lady Isabella was already infected.'

'How?'

Mary's nose twitches. 'She could smell it.'

'Don't be ridiculous. Your mother cannot smell the smallpox.'

'Yes, she can. If you had ever caught the merest hint of it, you'd never forget the stench. True enough, the next day Lady Isabella's throat began to blister so that she could not swallow. Mother made her a bed in our best parlour and nursed her tirelessly until the infection passed.'

'Lady Isabella resided at the parsonage?'

'For several weeks, yes.'

'With you?'

'Oh, no. Father took Martha and me to keep Christmas with his cousins in Tenby.'

'But you were immune?'

'So they claim. Yet my mother would not risk endangering her family by allowing us to sleep under the same roof as someone with the disease. She hardly dared enter the parlour while Lady Isabella was present.'

'Then how did she nurse her?' Jane has heard so much about Mrs Lloyd's direct contribution to Lady Isabella's salvation, she had imagined the woman standing over her, mopping her brow with a cold compress and forcing her to drink scalding broth as Jane's mother had done throughout her illness. However, it seems Mary has a very different understanding of what it means to nurse a dying patient back to health.

'She hung every red item of clothing we possessed about the sofa and pushed a tray through the door each morning.'

'*Red* items of clothing?'

'Yes. It's meant to expel the disease.'

'Can that possibly work?' Jane cannot remember anything about the colour red in Dr Jenner's pamphlet, but perhaps she should study it more thoroughly.

Mary shrugs. 'Well, I survived, so I suppose it must.'

'Why didn't you tell me before that Lady Isabella resided at Deane?'

'You never asked, and we had plenty of visitors in those days. We may have sunk in the world since Father died, but there was a time when we were considered worthy of receiving the very best families in Hampshire. Why, Lord Craven dined with us once, after joining the local hunt.' Mary sits taller, bristling with pride as she does whenever her mother's aristocratic cousin is mentioned. 'I don't see what any of this has to do with Mary Ellen. It was a full year after she went missing.'

'Probably nothing,' says Jane. But she does not believe in coincidences: they are the crutch of a lazy novelist. 'Would you consider inviting Lady Isabella to Edward's christening?'

'Do you think she'd come?'

'She might . . . for it is apparent she owes your family a vast debt of gratitude. And she has no heir of her own, you know. Ashe Park will go to Sir Robert's nearest male relation, but the fifty thousand pounds she inherited from the earl will be her own to dispose of.'

Mary looks to Mrs Austen for guidance. Happily, Jane can read her mother's machinations as easily as the hornbooks in her father's classroom. As James's eldest son, Edward will inherit all his father can afford to leave him – and still he is likely to be sorely lacking in fortune. 'Perhaps, my dear, you could invite her to stand as godmother.'

'If you really think it appropriate.'

'I'll fetch you some paper so that you may pen her a note,' says Jane. She cannot yet articulate *why* she is so keen to bring Mary face to face with Lady Isabella. Only that, instinct screams, the truth about what happened to Mary Ellen lies in whatever took place while her mother was residing with Mrs Lloyd.

LETTER 8

From Miss Jane Austen to Miss Austen

Steventon, 28 December 1798

My dearest Cassandra,

I don't believe I have ever thanked you for the kindness you showed to me during my illness in Southampton and I never will, since it is no more than your Christian duty. As the Good Lord has blessed you with a most extraordinarily benevolent temperament, it is only fair that he also sent you a sister whose very nature seems designed to provoke. What evidence of true goodness would your gentle smiles contain if I demanded no particular share of your attention? Indeed, I believe I begin to feel an ache in my throat, which I would be most grateful if you could attend to. Beth and her children can have no greater claim to your company, since they have each other but I have only you.

Yours petulantly,
J.A.

PS Tip the coachman handsomely for me and command him not to spare the horses.

Miss Austen
Edward Austen's Esqr
Godmersham Park
Faversham
Kent

LETTER 9

From Captain Henry Austen to
Miss Jane Austen

Ipswich, 27 December 1798

Dearest Jane,

From the postmark of this letter, you will already have guessed that the Oxfordshires remain impatient for orders to cross the Irish Sea. We have swelled our ranks by one hundred and fifty men and hold ourselves ready to march at the shortest notice yet we remain in East Anglia. During this time of enforced idleness, my wife has proved a boon to morale. Not just to myself, but to all my brother officers and their wives. Invitations to Eliza's musical gatherings are highly sought after and I flatter myself she is admired as the most graceful dancer at our weekly balls. Her previous incarnation, as the lady of a French officer, is quite forgotten. Or perhaps she is prized all the more for her defection. Remember poor Hastings in your prayers, I beg you, for he is weaker than ever.

I did not think much of the charade, or should I say the puzzle, you sent me. The button you sketched (very badly) is that of the 23rd Regiment of Foot, otherwise known as the Royal Welch Fusiliers, and in December 1782, the entire company would have been recovering from their defeat at Yorktown, before returning to Britain, along with the rest of His Majesty's troops, at the behest of General Washington. The three shapes above the '23' are ostrich feathers, as in the personal emblem of the Prince of Wales, not thistles, you ninny! Next time, leave the drawing to Cassy and send me your latest composition. Hang the postage! May I remind you that, although we may be satisfied that Elinor and Marianne get their just deserts, and First Impressions should never be relied on, Eliza and I remain anxious as to the fate of Lady Susan and her daughter. Will the vixen succeed in forming a match between Frederica and Sir James? Will Reginald be able to resist Lady Susan's charms? And will the young Vernons arrive at Parklands in time to restore Lady De Courcy's Christmas cheer? You must not quit there for, having read up to letter 41, I cannot tell if mother or daughter will prove the victor. As for my charade, if you guess the answer correctly, I promise to send you one:

> *You may lie on my first on the side of a stream,*
> *And my second compose to the nymph you adore,*
> *But if, when you've none of my whole, her esteem,*
> *And affection diminish – think of her no more!*

Yours impatiently,
Henry

ETONKNAB SI REWSNA EHT SP

Miss J. Austen
Steventon
Overton
Hants

Chapter Eleven

The next morning, Jane rises before the rest of her family and creeps unnoticed past a bleary-eyed Rosalee as the maid stands, brush and shovel in hand, weighing the merits of sweeping the grate against concealing yesterday's ashes beneath today's fire. On the doorstep, she pauses to read Henry's letter better in the daylight, blushing at her stupidity for not recognizing the royal emblem sooner but solving her brother's charade immediately. She cannot fathom why Henry is requesting a conclusion to *Lady Susan* now. It has been three years since Jane abandoned the work, unable to compose a resolution worthy of her wicked heroine. Confident his revelation will prove useful once she has had time to consider it, she tucks the note into her cape and continues her journey. The lane between the rectory and the rest of Steventon is alive with a cheerful riot of robins attempting to drown the more monotonous cry of the blackbird, but no other soul is present to witness Jane's unusually prompt appearance.

As she reaches the village, a dense frost covers the thatched roofs of the cottages, creating a picturesque impression of a county built entirely from sugar plums. Smoke rises from but one of the red-brick chimneys. After a lifetime spent tending other women's infants, including Jane and all her siblings, Dame Culham is an early riser. Rather than risk disturbing the row of icicles hanging from the eaves over the front of the property, Jane passes through the neatly kept garden and lets herself into the kitchen. The cluttered space, with its bundles of dried herbs hanging from the low-beamed ceiling and oversized brick fireplace, is as familiar to Jane as her own bedroom.

Within it, her former nurse stands with her sloped back to the door, humming softly as she pours water from a steaming kettle into an earthenware teapot. Jane's brother, Georgy, sits at the scrubbed-pine table, contemplating a plate of generously buttered rolls before him. His hazel eyes flash in recognition at her entrance. After setting her basket beside him, she kisses his cheek. His morning whiskers are sharp against her lips.

Dame Culham does not so much as raise an eyebrow when she turns to find an extra chair at her table has been occupied. 'Early for you. Is it not?' she says, in a tone that implies Jane is a sluggard.

Jane lifts the lid of the pot to see what's inside. Dame Culham does not believe in paying for tea to be imported from China when dandelion and burdock grow freely along the base of the hedgerow. Sure enough, dried green leaves float on the surface. Jane wrinkles her nose and replaces the lid, determining not to accept a cup. She does not bother to rebut the accusation. Anyone would be a sluggard compared to her former nurse. As well as caring for Georgy, she is the only trained midwife for miles around. Her profession leaves her vulnerable to being summoned at all times of day and night to assist women in their labours, and she is often appointed to the unenviable task of laying out the dead. If Jane is to identify the skeleton before the ground thaws and it is tipped into the communal grave at Deane, burying the truth for ever, she must confront the horrors she fled from that day in Deane. Dame Culham is the only person who might be willing, and able, to help her interpret the remains.

'I come bearing gifts.' Jane nods towards the basket, which Georgy has already ferreted through to retrieve his mother's spiced gingerbread.

'I'm not in want of your charity.' Dame Culham sniffs at the remaining parcel, wrapped in brown paper and tied with string.

'It's not charity, it's a Christmas present.' Jane takes it from her basket and slides it across the table. Still, Dame Culham eyes the gift as if accepting it would be tantamount to throwing herself on the parish. After a few moments, she reluctantly pulls the string loose and unwraps the paper to reveal a neatly folded linen shift. 'I would never condescend to offer you charity, Nan,' Jane says, employing the familiar name all the Austen children use to revere her. 'Especially as I hear you've had plenty of work of late. Preparing the remains James found in the cellar at Deane for burial must have been a macabre task. I hope he compensated you well for it?'

'So that's why you're here, is it?' Dame Culham shakes the linen loose and holds it up to the low morning light, streaming through the glazed window. She nods approvingly at the neat hem, and Jane cannot help but feel a swell of pride.

'And to wish you both the compliments of the season. I would have called in sooner, only the weather has been so poor and I've been busy. James and Mary have been staying with us at the rectory, and I've been helping to care for Anna and Edward . . .' She trails off. Dame Culham will have no patience with Jane's reasons for neglecting to visit Georgy thus far over Christmas.

'How is the new mother?'

'Well, I believe.' Is Mary well? Jane finds she must ask herself. 'She seems to have taken rather a long time to recover from the birth and she fusses terribly over the baby, but she has finally agreed to be churched.'

'That's only to be expected.' A recently delivered woman is possibly the only species Dame Culham has any sympathy for. 'As for yourself, I've been wondering what was keeping you.' She offers Jane a sly smile, and Jane feels a crackle of electricity pass between them. Dame Culham is not fooled by the mask of politeness Jane wears to hide her curiosity from most people. She will know Jane's true reason for calling.

'Where are the remains now?' Jane glances around the kitchen, as if there might be a small coffin beneath the linen press.

'With your brother.'

'Oh . . .'

'As I said, I might have expected you earlier. It's been almost a fortnight since Jack brought them to me.'

Jane balls her fists, digging her fingernails into the palms of her hands in frustration. If only she had thought to come to Dame Culham directly. She might have allowed her to stand witness as she prepared the remains for burial. Jane could try searching All Saints for the coffin and prising it open to view the contents. Without anyone to own the deceased or pay for a coffin, she knows the custom is to store the corpse in the church box and tip it into the bare earth of the communal grave after the service. But Dame Culham will have already enclosed the shroud. Jane might be confident in her ability to unpick it and sew it up again without anyone noticing, but even if she had the stomach to commit such an act, she is quite sure it would be blasphemy. 'What of the clothes they were wrapped in?'

'I burned them.'

Jane's last hope was that Mrs Terry, or even Mary, might recognize one of the articles, if only she could lay her hands on it. 'Even the buttons?'

Dame Culham hardens her jaw. 'Are you accusing me of stealing from the dead, Jane?'

'Of course not. But do you really have nothing left at all?'

'Mr Craven has the buttons. The rest I threw onto the fire.'

Jane rubs her temples, furious with herself. 'Oh, Nan, what am I to do? Mr Craven has declared the corpse is that of a vagrant soldier. But I earnestly believe it's a woman and, unless I can prove it before they bury her as such, she'll never be at peace.'

'She was a female, all right.'

'You concur?' Jane sits up in her seat, bolstered by the relief of being believed, at last.

'I do.'

'Was it the white silk that made you believe so? I thought it might have been a shift, or a nightdress?'

'No, it was her holy-bone and pelvis. They were too wide to belong to a man.'

'Oh . . .' Jane falters. She has been schooled not to discuss intimate areas of one's person. She cannot imagine the licence it would take to handle them so freely as to determine the sex. 'Well, I did not see her skeleton, only her head and her clothing. Did you tell Mr Craven?'

'No.'

'Why not?'

'I did not consider it any of my business. Your brother tasked me with preparing the remains for burial, so that was what I did.'

'But how am I to find her murderer, if I cannot prove who she is?'

'You will not find her murderer.'

Jane's heart sags. She hoped she might have found an ally in Dame Culham, but even she doubts her ability to solve this mystery. 'I know it's been many years, and it may be supremely difficult to bring the guilty party to justice, but if I can show that the victim is not who the magistrate believes she is, he might take my investigation into who murdered her more seriously.'

Dame Culham clicks her tongue, impatiently. 'You will not find her murderer because she was not *murdered*.'

'But . . .'

'You say you saw her head?'

'Briefly.'

'And did you not notice anything strange about the skin?'

'Apart from it being mummified?'

Dame Culham frowns. She does not care for Jane's sarcasm. 'Describe it to me.'

'Describe it?'

'Yes. You, who are so good with words, describe her skin to me. Tell me, in as much detail as you can stand to, exactly what you saw.'

'Well . . .' Jane squeezes her eyes shut and recalls the shock of meeting with the woman's shrivelled features in the pantry. She is tired of berating herself for being unable to examine the findings in a calm, rational manner. It would have been very different for Dame Culham. Jack would have warned her about the advanced stage of decomposition, and she will have already seen scores of corpses in her line of work, while Jane was entirely unprepared for the gruesome sight that awaited her. 'It was discoloured, stretched across her features.'

'Go on.' Dame Culham nods encouragingly, as she did when Jane first began to repeat the names of the various animals surrounding her in the Hampshire countryside. 'How else could you describe it?'

'Almost blue . . .' Jane places both hands on her cheeks, pulling her own skin taut over her skull '. . . and mottled.'

'Mottled, yes. And did you not think that strange?'

'Not particularly. But I'd never made the acquaintance of a mummified head before.'

Dame Culham narrows her eyes. 'Those were pustules, Jane. Her face, her scalp, the backs of her hands any remaining bits of skin were riddled with them.'

'Pustules . . . as in the smallpox?' Jane gasps in realization. All this time she has been trying to work out what had happened to Mary Ellen when the answer was staring her in the face. 'Oh, Nan! I must take leave.' She grabs her former nurse's cheeks between her hands and kisses her forehead as Georgy looks on, amused.

'Be gone with you.' Dame Culham swats away Jane's embrace, but even she is laughing. It is the same throaty laugh as when Jane, as a child, would climb onto her lap and whisper her childish nonsense into her ear.

Chapter Twelve

It takes Jane less than an hour to walk to Ashe from Steventon. The morning is suspended in limbo. Whenever her path takes her in reach of the pale sunlight, she could close her eyes and almost believe that spring was fast approaching. Yet, in the unforgiving shade of Hampshire's dense hedgerows and rolling hills, hoar frost smothers the fallen leaves, grass and ivy underfoot, and the wind blows with such ferocity she fears it could slice her to the bone.

As she reaches the farm, a pair of maids stand beside the brick dairy, exhausted by their early-morning endeavours. Both women ignore her as they lift their yokes onto their broad shoulders. Jane notes the strength required to bear the weight of two enormous pails each. Mrs Chute's chip construction, so daintily set upon her head, seems a cruel mockery of their honest labours. She catches her breath as she crosses paths with Mr Bolton, driving a herd of softly mooing cows back to pasture. The elderly man touches his hat and peers at her quizzically. Jane lifts her chin and scurries past, hoping her confident manner will discourage him from enquiring as to why she is cutting through his fields to reach the mansion. She cannot risk the farmer guessing the purpose of her visit and alerting its inhabitants.

Several long minutes later, she locates the narrow gap in the overgrown privet hedge, which separates park from farmland, and emerges into an icy garden. Jane suspects the area was once the head gardener's pride and joy, crowded with topiary clipped into pristine shapes to be admired from the windows above. Now, each monstrous tower of yew is deformed beyond all recognition, and the carefully planted knots of box are all but hidden beneath a tangle of brambles. A stubborn frost cloaks the indistinguishable forms as the entire parterre is shielded from the gentle light of the mid-morning sun by the long shadow of Ashe House. Jane shivers as she surveys its wilfully neglected façade, the decorative brickwork choked by vines and the wooden shutters rotting from their hinges, contemplating how she might summon the mistress of this decay without allowing her time to prepare.

But Jane is in luck as she stands, motionless. A slight figure, wrapped in a sable-trimmed pelisse and tethered to two wayward pugs, steps out from behind an ivy-clad pillar onto the glittering York-stone path. She is less than fifty feet away, the opposite side of a rectangular pond, encrusted with ice and choked with dead reeds. 'Come, come, you naughty boys. Do your business so Mamma can go and snooze in front of the fire.'

'Pray, wait,' Jane calls, her voice startlingly loud, even to herself.

'Who goes there?' The woman recoils, instinctively reaching for her hood and pulling it low over her face.

Jane takes quick steps towards her. 'Be not alarmed. It is I, Miss Austen.'

'No, do not be so cruel as to look when I am unveiled.' She whirls around, speeding towards the house and dragging the dogs behind her. But Jane is determined not to release her until she has extracted the truth of what became of Lady Isabella's disobliging daughter.

'Wait, please . . . Miss Portal!'

The woman halts, turning her head a fraction but holding the fur in place to conceal her features. '*What* did you call me?'

'Mary Ellen . . .' This is the truth that Jane has come to Ashe Park with which to assail its mistress. 'It is you, isn't it? That's why you hide your face, so that you may masquerade as Lady Isabella and claim the fortune your mother so cruelly deprived you of.'

'How dare you?' she splutters, voice trembling with fury. 'Your father shall hear of this. I might have expected more respect, nay, more pity, from a clergyman's daughter. And you, who have borne witness to my ravaged hands. How can you be so unfeeling as to doubt my countenance is thus afflicted?'

'Because it is not Venetian ceruse you have to thank for your recovery. Your complexion remains relatively unscathed as you were never so severely afflicted. Your hands were marred by the cowpox, *not* the smallpox.' It was the difference between poor Mary's blighted complexion and the light, silvery patches on Mrs Terry's skin that had first led Jane to question 'Lady Isabella's' account of her suffering. After consulting Dr Jenner's pamphlet, she is confident that cowpox pustules can be severe and lead to lasting scars, but they are not as profuse as those of the smallpox and, most importantly, they do not spread to the face.

'Ridiculous!' She snorts. 'How could anyone believe it possible for a lady of my rank to contract such a low, vulgar disease?'

'Because you managed the dairy, and it's terribly contagious. All it would have taken was for you to pick up a spoon or pail that had been handled by one who was infected.'

'And you are an expert on such matters, are you?'

'Well, I finally read Dr Jenner's *Inquiry*.' Jane cringes at the precociousness of her tone. 'It's really very interesting.'

'Very well, but you cannot read me.' The woman darts towards the house but the flagstones are cracked and slippery with ice and, unlike Jane who is wearing walking boots, she is unprepared for such treacherous terrain in her silk slippers. The pugs yap in protest, their sharp claws flailing on the frozen ground. She pauses to pull them closer, preventing the dogs from skittering into the pond.

'It grants one immunity to its deadly cousin,' Jane calls after her. 'Perhaps you knew that, when you returned to the park to nurse Cecilia and Augusta. Or perhaps your love for your sisters was so great, you did not think twice about endangering your own life to care for them.' At the mention of Cecilia and Augusta, the woman's shoulders rise and fall with a pitiful heaviness. She is still winded by the shock of losing her sisters, even after all these years. 'In your parting note, you told your mother you'd rather work for your bread than become a wife, and you did. Not as a governess or a lady's companion, or any other position where you might have been recognized as the daughter of Lady Isabella and Sir Robert but as a dairy maid. For the entire period you've been missing, you've been hiding beneath our very noses . . . on your own farm for the first twelve months?'

'This is preposterous.'

'No, it's not. Cecilia managed the dairy after you. She would have kept you hidden. And I suspect you might even have had Mr Bolton in your thrall.' The woman flinches at what Jane assumes is the truth of her words. She can just imagine a young Mary Ellen, crying on Mr Bolton's lap at the injustice of her fate. What would a sympathetic man, such as her own father, not agree to in order to dry the tears of one he had looked on as a daughter? 'That's why Mr Chute's hounds could not trace you any further than the estate. You never left, not initially. But no one thought to look for you on the farm. Who could anticipate the granddaughter of an earl would choose the life of a dairy maid over mistress of The Vyne?'

'Really, Miss Austen. The very notion is ridiculous.'

'Cecilia and Augusta were found in bed, their faces covered by a sheet. Which means someone had tended them upon their deaths . . .' By now, Jane is so close she is tempted to reach out a hand to touch the woman's shoulder to prevent her from getting away. But she does not yet know what this woman is capable of, and if she retaliates, Jane may find herself skidding into the icy pond. 'The household were in no position to care for them. Sir Robert was the first to succumb, and Lady Isabella had deserted her daughters, which means it could only have been you.'

'Stop this, I beg you.' Her voice turns from an angry hiss into a heaving sob.

But Jane's conscience will not allow her to desist until she has extracted the truth. 'Then, on Christmas Day, you went to Deane. Mrs Lloyd believed Lady Isabella had lost her wits, that she was decrying your spirit in her delirium but it *was* you she overheard her arguing with through the door. You murdered your mother, hid her remains in the cellar and took her place in her sickbed so you could claim her fortune.'

'Enough!' She turns so abruptly her hood falls away, revealing a countenance so pert that Jane can be in no doubt of her identity. With her heart-shaped face and the tear-filled eyes of such beguiling blue they are almost violet, Mary Ellen is every bit as beautiful as Mrs Terry described. 'I murdered *no one*. It was *my* life that was so unfairly taken from me!'

Jane draws back, electrified by the sensation of being proved correct in her suspicions. She must seize this moment to learn everything she can. 'Then tell me, what did happen? How did your mother's body come to rest in a cellar for all these years?'

Mary Ellen glances both ways, as if she cannot quite believe Jane has goaded her into revealing herself so readily. 'I went to the parsonage to make peace with my mother, not to kill her. As you guessed, my father was dead and I had already nursed Cecilia and Augusta through their final moments. Mamma and I were all that was left of our family, and still, she refused to recognize me.'

Jane sincerely hopes she is not so shallow as to be blinded by Mary Ellen's pretty face. It is an awful coincidence that Lady Isabella should die of her affliction the same night that Mary Ellen revealed herself. 'If you did not kill Lady Isabella, then how did she come to die at the very moment you returned?'

'She perished, as she lived, from spite.' Mary Ellen juts out her pointed chin, refusing to be cowed. 'My mother used her final breath to curse me, after I had come to share my condolences and offer my services as a nurse. I had thought, foolishly, that our grief might unite us – but she was so angry it sent her into a fit of apoplexy. There was nothing I could do to placate her.

Everything I told you was the truth of what she said to me that night. She blamed me for all of our family's misfortunes.'

Mary Ellen may inadvertently have speeded Lady Isabella's passing with her reappearance, but Jane is tempted to believe she did not cause it. If what Mary said was true, she may even have spared her mother from the prolonged agony of death by the smallpox. 'And so, with Mrs Lloyd determined to keep herself out of her ladyship's way, you wrapped her corpse in the items meant to dispel the disease and dumped it in the cellar before climbing into her sickbed?' After a year of manual labour, Mary Ellen would have possessed the strength required to drag the corpse to the pantry and prise open the trapdoor. Only someone who was confident they were immune to the disease would dare lie between the sheets of a smallpox sufferer. She cannot say where Mrs Lloyd obtained the pauper's cloak. Perhaps it belonged to a servant, but the regimental jacket of the Welch Fusiliers *must* have belonged to a relative of the Welshman, Mr Lloyd.

'What other choice had I? I needed to make the arrangements for Cecilia and Augusta to be laid to rest. I had no designs on my father's estate or my mother's fortune. It was guardianship of my sisters that I desired. And as Mary Ellen, I had already been cut out from the family so was as good as dead in the eyes of the law.'

It is true. Mary Ellen has not installed herself at the park and does not seek benefit from her mother's position in society. As far as Jane can tell, since her family were cut down, she has lived as a nomad, wandering from place to place and withdrawing only the funds necessary to sustain herself. 'And Mr Bolton? Did you purchase his silence with the lease for Ashe Farm?'

'Leave Mr Bolton aside. He is an innocent in all this.'

Jane doubts Mary Ellen could have remained hidden in the dairy for a full year, or changed places with her dead mother, without the assistance of at least one member of the household. If the estate had been transferred to Sir Robert's nearest male relation, rather than remaining in control of Mary Ellen posing as Lady Isabella, Mr Bolton might have lost his home and his livelihood. Instead, he has been elevated to the position of prosperous tenant farmer while her crimes have remained undetected. Jane cannot help but suspect these two circumstances are linked. 'And, still, I find it most suspicious that you allow the park to fall to ruin while securing the most conscientious tenant for the farm.'

'There are many who rely on the farm for their living' – Mary Ellen turns to the ruined façade – 'but this house is nothing short of a mausoleum. Before I die, I shall see it razed to the ground.'

Regardless, Jane is not here to argue for the upkeep of the mansion or on behalf of Sir Robert's heir. When she began this investigation, her aim was to establish the identity of whoever had been discarded in the cellar so that they might be remembered and laid to rest with dignity. Lady Isabella was certainly a cruel and spiteful mother, but that does not give Mary Ellen the right to conceal her death and consign her to an unmarked grave. 'You cannot maintain this fiction for ever. I understand that, in your grief, you may have panicked and hidden your mother's body. But now that her remains have been unearthed, you must see it's time for you to confess. Lady Isabella deserves to rest with dignity.'

'La! She deserves nothing after she sold me, like a Southdown sheep. I begged with her to release me from the engagement to Mr Chute. Instead, she kept me prisoner until after the ceremony, threatening to marry Cecilia or Augusta to him if I refused.'

'So that's why you went through with the marriage, to spare your sisters from a similar fate.' It is the one part of the mystery that Jane has thus far been unable to fathom. Mary Ellen really would have done anything for her sisters.

'Yes. But, afterwards, I found my spirit rebelled at all attempts to subdue it. I could not, in all good conscience, stand up with Mr Chute as his bride.'

'Why? What was so terrible about William Chute?'

Mary Ellen narrows her eyes at the stupidity of Jane's question. 'About William himself, nothing. He is no worse, and certainly no better, than any other man of my acquaintance. They are all weak, contemptible creatures. But it was the station of a wife I found most objectionable. You may be the kind of young lady who is so full of milkiness as to pledge her obedience to another without hesitation, but *I* am not.'

Jane knows she should be repulsed by Mary Ellen's admissions, but her respect for her rises. 'Returning to Lady Isabella. As a Christian, she deserves a decent burial . . .'

'What kind of Christian refuses to grant forgiveness, even on their deathbed?' A flicker of victory crosses Mary Ellen's satisfied features, as Jane struggles to compose a rational reply. 'If I am an unnatural daughter, then it is because I am the product of a most unnatural mother. But tell me, Miss Austen, how did you know?'

Jane sighs as she casts her eyes down at Romulus and Remus, both panting at the sheer effort of sniffing Mary Ellen's slippers. 'Apart from anything else, from everything I've heard about Lady Isabella, I cannot see her giving house room to two blind, incontinent pugs.'

Mary Ellen barks a short laugh. 'How astute you are! My mother cared even less for animals than she did for children, but sickness disgusted her most of all. Cecilia and Augusta had only just broken out in the first pustules when she abandoned them . . .' A door creaks and Mary Ellen's menacing attendant steps out onto the terrace, interrupting her speech. He looks between the two women, and Jane senses he has been watching, waiting to be summoned to intervene on his mistress's behalf. Mary Ellen replaces her hood, and the atmosphere turns as icy as their surroundings. 'Miss Austen was just leaving, Wilson. I'd be grateful if you could escort her as far as the lane.'

'But . . .' Jane attempts to protest. She may have solved the mystery of whom the remains belonged to, but she has failed to bring about any fitting resolution for Lady Isabella.

'Go and never return. Neither you nor your truths are welcome here. If you dare repeat the particulars of our conversation, I shall bring you before a judge for slander and accuse you of being most cruel to a sick, grieving old lady.' Mary Ellen's bow-shaped lips form a wry smile, and Jane cannot escape the sensation that she has rather enjoyed their exchange. However much she is determined to remain hidden, it must be a relief to be seen, even for a brief moment, for the woman she really is.

LETTER 10

From Mrs Eliza Austen, the Dowager Comtesse de Feuillide, to Miss Jane Austen

Ipswich, 30 December 1798

I will not attempt, My Dear Cousin, nay, Sister, to make you any apology for not having sooner answered your kind letter, since I trust you're too well convinced of my affection to resent me for my silence. It is often said that matrimony robs one of one's correspondents, and since I entrusted my hand to your dear brother, I have had little time to take up a pen. Indeed, each evening, my new commander has me sing myself hoarse and play my harp until my fingers bleed, for he says the fate of the entire regiment, nay, all the King's men, depends upon me! I wish you would oblige my requests to join us here at camp, if only for a few weeks, for there are so many dashing young men I would be in raptures to see you stand up with.

You claim my aunt could not possibly spare you while Cassandra is away, but surely there is a neighbour or some other person who could remain with her? Perhaps our mutual cousin, Philly, would do? She is quite the country mouse and would not mind coming to you instead of me, for life at camp really is very gay! Likely far too gay for Philly. Tell me you agree, and I will turn Philly's coach to Steventon the moment it arrives. Even my dear little Hastings is proving a most dedicated recruit. His new pappa presented him with a battalion of toy soldiers for Christmas, and he spends all day lining them up for battle upon his tray and laying waste to Bonaparte from his sickbed. What a mighty general he will make when he is grown!

Now to address your enquiry before my duties to the King force me to conclude. I did make the acquaintance of a Lady Isabella (or possibly Isabel or Isadore) at Vichy in the winter of '84, or maybe '85. Hastings had not yet arrived, and my dear mamma remained by my side. Regardless, she cannot be the same lady you mention, as she was the most bewitching creature I ever saw. True, I do not remember her hands, as brightly coloured kid gloves were very much in vogue at the time (mine were canary yellow and paired beautifully with my chemise à la reine. I must find them to show you . . .), but her face and neck were the most brilliant white. She travelled with a prodigiously handsome, if rather coarse, young man whom she claimed was her attendant but the French ladies, with their sinful imaginations, insisted that was merely a euphemism.

Adieu, My Dear Jane, do not be so petty as to let my tardiness prevent you from writing to me often, and promise me you will find some other drudge to entertain your mother and come to me soon — for even I cannot hope to satisfy so many officers all by myself!

Your ever devoted,
Eliza

Miss J. Austen
Steventon
Overton
Hants

Chapter Thirteen

New Year's Day arrives without Jane having reached a conclusion as to how she may resolve the matter of Mary Ellen's crimes to the satisfaction of the law and her own conscience. It is difficult to believe that a woman in possession of enough human kindness to risk her life to nurse her dying sisters could wilfully commit murder, whereas Lady Isabella's last will and testament is living proof of her spiteful, unforgiving nature. That Mary Ellen is guilty of concealing her death, and of posing as Lady Isabella to claim her fortune, is indisputable but the money she stole was that which she was unfairly disqualified from inheriting by a malicious mother who sought to dominate, then rub out her daughter's life.

However much Jane fears it would be unchristian of her to allow Lady Isabella to languish unnamed in a pauper's grave, in exposing Mary Ellen's wrongdoings she would risk an unsympathetic judge sending her to the scaffold, condemn Mr Chute as a bigamist and shatter the peace of the second Mrs Chute. Jane may not care for the company of Elizabeth Chute, but she bears her no malice; and while the young William Chute cannot be said to have behaved particularly well towards his first wife, he is hardly the cruellest species of husband in England. It is not uncommon for a person to marry after being persuaded in their affections by those parties whose interest is best secured in bringing about the match. A man's pride would rather interpret a woman's reticence as modesty, than believe her indifferent towards him.

Thankfully, the unrelenting cold gives Jane licence to deliberate. As a fresh sprinkling of frost is cast over Hampshire each bitter winter morning, and the earth steadfastly refuses to thaw, Jane prevaricates between revulsion at the depths of Mary Ellen's self-preservation and a begrudging admiration of her audacity. While there is no possibility of the remains being buried, Jane can afford to maintain her silence. She knows she must come to a decision soon, however, and the responsibility of deciding Mary Ellen's fate bears down on her. It is as burdensome as the embrace of Mary on one side and her mother on the other, as the trio climb the lane between the rectory and St Nicholas's for Edward's christening.

'Slow down, dear,' says Mrs Austen, as the pointed spire of the church appears above the treetops. 'It's not a race.'

Jane squints at the white sky, stark against the barren branches of oak and hawthorn. 'No, but we should not keep Mary and Edward in the cold any longer than we must.'

'I told Austen we should have taken the carriage.' Mary's cheeks redden, whether with pique or exertion Jane cannot tell.

James, cradling his infant son in one hand while attempting to restrain Anna with the other, sighs wearily. 'The carriage is already loaded with our belongings, and the ceremony will not take long. We shall all be resting in front of a roaring fire before you know it. I left instructions with Rosalee to maintain a good flame.'

'Why, the slattern will have been half asleep in my chair as soon as we left! And we cannot begin the ceremony until Lady Isabella arrives.' Despite having received no response to her invitation, Mary has become so enraptured with the idea that Lady Isabella will accept, in acknowledgement of the great debt she bears Mrs Lloyd, that she will consider it her duty to stand as Edward's godmother and, moreover, the highest honour, bequeath him her entire fortune.

'I fear the weather may keep her within doors for she is an invalid, after all,' says Jane, wishing to temper Mary's disappointment. She had hoped that by encouraging Mary to invite Lady Isabella to the christening she might save herself the trouble of exposing Mary Ellen by letting her relations do it. Her mother and father, Mary and even James were acquainted with Lady Isabella and her daughter. If Jane could gather them all in close proximity, and contrive a way of lifting the lady's veil, then surely they would recognize her. But as Mary Ellen has evidently taken some trouble to mix only in those circles where Lady Isabella was unknown before her illness, Jane doubts she will risk appearing today. Especially now that she knows Jane is privy to her lies.

'Not her ladyship.' Mary will not be dissuaded from her plans for her son's future. 'She would not be denied a carriage, and I expect she's most eager to meet Edward.' She smiles fondly at her son as she retrieves him from his father.

Freed of the child, James disappears beneath the branches of the ancient yew beside the entrance to the church. Rather than carry the enormous key home to the rectory after every service, and risk his wife tidying it away, Mr Austen keeps it hidden in the tree's hollow trunk. Anna scrambles after him, delighted by this grown-up game of hide-and-seek. When she emerges, bonnet askew and twigs lodged in her ringlets, the little girl is brandishing the key between both hands as a prize. She carries it, with much self-import, to her grandfather.

'Thank you, my dear.' Mr Austen places it inside the cast-iron lock of the arched door, and turns, but the mechanism refuses to budge. 'I fear it may be frozen.'

'Be gentle!' says Mrs Austen, as her husband continues to rattle the key 'Whatever you do, don't jam the key in. That would be all we need.'

'Wait!' says Mary, as the lock finally springs free. 'I

think I hear a carriage.' She casts her eyes down the lane with such hope that Jane is sorry for ever having raised her expectations.

'It's probably the mail coach arriving at the Wheatsheaf Inn.' Mr Austen dismisses Mary's ambitions.

But James leans his head to the side. 'No, Mary's right. That is a carriage approaching.'

After an agonizing minute or two of doubt, a pair of chestnut mares crests the hill, puffing clouds of condensation into the frigid air as their muscles ripple beneath their glossy coats. Behind them, a bright yellow chaise creaks and groans in protest at being dragged up the steep incline. To Jane's astonishment, the driver, riding postillion and bundled against the cold in a tattered greatcoat and three-cornered hat, is Lady Isabella's attendant. He turns the carriage in a full circle, coming to a halt before the awestruck family.

'I told you she'd come,' says Mary, as the passenger, her face concealed by a turquoise veil and the hood of a sable-trimmed pelisse, flips open the window.

'Your ladyship?' Mr Austen advances, as James bows and Mary, Mrs Austen and even Anna curtsey. Jane can sense, rather than see, the woman smirk as she is forced, by the rules of decorum and her own timidity, to follow suit. From Mary Ellen's smug composure and reluctance to exit the carriage, Jane cannot tell if she has come to confess her sins or taunt her with her audacity.

'Mr Austen, I wish to express my gratitude to you

for your part in managing my trust. I'm afraid it must have been quite an inconvenience to you all these years, and I'm glad to have relieved you of it.'

'Not at all, ma'am. Anything to oblige a neighbour.'

'Good, because I come to impose on you further. You will deliver this contribution to Mrs Lefroy's cause.' She drops a banknote of fifty pounds out of the carriage, as if it is worth no more than a handbill.

'Certainly, ma'am.' Mr Austen is preserved from having to scrabble around in the dirt by the enthusiastic assistance of Anna, who catches the note before it is blown down the hill.

'And one more thing . . . the skeleton your son uncovered beneath Deane Parsonage.'

'Yes?' Mr Austen replies, and Jane can feel her father's attention wander from the lady to her. Has Mary Ellen come to reveal the corpse's true identity before making her escape, now that she is in full control of her mother's fifty thousand pounds?

'I'd like you to inter it here, at Steventon.'

'You would?'

'Yes. Something Miss Austen said to me made me realize I cannot rule out the possibility it is that of my errant daughter. And, if so, it is only right that she should rest beside her sisters.'

'Of course, ma'am.' Mr Austen bows again. 'Would you like me to arrange to have Mary Ellen's name added to the inscription, too.'

'Oh, no, there's no need to go to that trouble,' she

replies, without hesitating. Mr Austen can only look to his family in reply, bewildered by her callous attitude. Jane is forced to choke down a laugh. 'Well then, adieu!'

'Wait!' cries Jane, finally gaining the temerity to approach the carriage. 'Are you not joining us inside St Nicholas's?'

'What for?'

'James Edward's christening,' she explains, as Mary lifts her son to the window, so that his prospective god-mother may better admire him.

'Oh, yes . . . the child's christening.' Mary Ellen reaches out to stroke the baby's cheek. The pugs, sensing competition for their mistress's affection, yip and snarl on her lap and Mary quickly draws her baby back to her breast. 'No, I'm afraid I really don't think I can. I must away, for I have a ship to catch, and I fear the weather is about to turn for the worse.' Her voice wavers as she raises her eyes to the church and, with a pang, Jane realizes she cannot bear to look upon the graves of Cecilia and Augusta. 'But not to worry, *you* may be my proxy.' Mary Ellen levels a finger at Jane. 'You will oblige me, won't you, Miss Austen?'

Mary Ellen is too clever not to know that by asking Jane to sign the parish register on behalf of Lady Isabella she is making her an accomplice to her crimes. And yet, for once, Jane cannot find the words to object. It is not that her courage fails her. Rather, until Twelfth Night, it remains the season of Christmastide, the time of year when the veil between the living and the dead is at its thinnest. Who is Jane to declare this apparition is not Lady Isabella, or that Mary Ellen has not passed temporarily into a realm of the dead? 'As you wish, ma'am.' She curtseys, in exaggerated deference, while refusing to lower her gaze from the veiled figure.

'Excellent. You may also select a gift of plate from my collection at the park. Mr Bolton will grant you access and show you where it is kept.'

'Oh, how kind!' Mary beams at her son's new benefactress.

Jane smiles, too, but she fears her expression has a rictus edge. Not satisfied with implicating her in her deception, Mary Ellen is tasking Jane with carrying away stolen goods.

'Very well. All that remains is for me to wish you the compliments of the season.' She slams the window shut and thumps the side of her fist on the roof, ordering her attendant to drive without waiting for the family's reply.

'She hasn't changed a bit,' says Mary, as the family huddle together to watch the carriage descend until it is out of sight.

Jane cannot help but look at her sister-in-law askance. 'Really? Are you certain of that?'

'Yes, for she has always been on the most intimate terms with our family. Be sure to select something substantial from Ashe, won't you? Don't come back with an eggcup if there's a serving platter to be had. Remember, it's in your nephew's interest.'

'I promise I shall take the largest piece of silver I can carry,' replies Jane, haunted by the old proverb that one might as well be hanged for a sheep as a lamb. 'Although I fear her ladyship's generosity will be wasted on Mrs Lefroy, for I cannot see anyone hereabouts being the first to volunteer for Dr Jenner's procedure.'

'Why, she will begin with Edward.' Mary holds the baby tighter in her arms. 'Once people know the vicar's son has been granted immunity in such a way, they will not be afraid of the consequences.'

'Are we not afraid of the consequences?' asks James. From the look of alarm on his features, it is clear this is one of the few decisions Mary has not referred to her husband.

'I shouldn't care if he sprouts horns and his first word is "moo". If it spares him from the horrors Lady Isabella and I suffered, it will have been worth it.'

Jane lays a hand on Mary's shoulder. 'Sometimes, Mary, you are very wise.'

'What do you mean, "sometimes"? Am I not always wise?'

'We should go in. It's snowing,' Jane replies, as her family tactfully avoid meeting her gaze.

To her great surprise, it really is snowing. The crystals descend slowly, like goose down dancing in the breeze, coming to rest in fluffy mounds all around. Anna shrieks, sticking out her tongue and spinning in circles to catch the falling flakes. Even the branches of the ancient yew are outstretched to greet them, and soon the tree is cloaked in a shimmering coat of white. The family pause to admire the majestic sight, before entering St Nicholas's and gathering beside the stone font. As usual, Jane is drawn to the two cherubs decorating the memorial to Cecilia and Augusta Portal. As she moves instinctively towards it, her father comes to her side. 'Will you let me know once you've interred her?' she asks. She will need to pray to the Good Lord, and possibly Lady Isabella, for forgiveness for her complicity in Mary Ellen's schemes every time she sits in this pew from now on.

Mr Austen looks rueful. 'I already have. She lies directly below where you are standing.' Jane shifts her weight. The floor moves with her. Her father must have lifted it to bury the remains directly beneath the plaque. 'I hope that will be an end to the matter.'

'Yes,' Jane replies, after a long moment's consideration. 'I think it will have to be.' She stares at the flagstone, worn smooth by centuries of worshippers, wondering if Mary Ellen's request was a sign her heart had softened towards her mother or if banishing Lady Isabella to spend eternity beside the daughters she had abandoned is her final act of revenge. In death, at least, they will not be divided.

Mr Austen sighs, shoulders sloping. 'Your entreaties have encouraged me to examine my conscience, and I fear I did not perform my Christian duty towards Mary Ellen as well as I might have. I sincerely hope, if those are her remains, that she will be at peace.' Jane bites her lip. Her father does not need to know that by dissolving the trust and hiding Lady Isabella's corpse, he, like her, has done quite enough to afford Mary Ellen peace. 'Now, how would you like to enter the details of Edward's christening into the register?'

'Me?'

'Yes. For, as I am learning, your word is as good as mine.'

'Then I'd be delighted to.' Jane's heart swells at being entrusted to announce the birth of the latest Austen to the world. Her family may squabble and bicker and drive her to distraction, but they are united. Not only by love and faith, but by a determination to embrace each other, despite their many foibles. There is possibly no other family in England that could tolerate her relentless desire to be the author of her own story, never mind encourage her tenacious curiosity or take pride in her occasional brilliance. Jane could never forsake her place among them, not even to live as freely as Mary Ellen.

To be continued . . .

Author's Note

As usual, I hope the reader will forgive me for taking such enormous liberties with the lives of Jane Austen and her friends, family and acquaintances, especially in this season of goodwill.

Austen is thought to have written the epistolary section of *Lady Susan* (another Christmas novella, to which *The Austen Christmas Murders* pay homage) between 1794 and 1795, and added the conclusion several years later when she made a fair copy of the manuscript to send to her niece.

'Charades' in Austen's time referred to a parlour game in which participants guessed words from a description set to a three-part verse or play (the first two denote a syllable, while the last describes the word). All the charades included here were composed by members of the Austen family and the answers can be found written backwards at the bottom of each letter (another Austen tradition!).

James Edward Austen Leigh was christened at All Saints church, Deane, on 1 January 1799. Austen entered the details into the parish register herself, thereby recording the birth of her first biographer, whose efforts to document her life and the family's fond recollections of 'Aunt Jane' we have to thank as the founding source of all subsequent biographies.

Mary Lloyd's father, Reverend Noyes Lloyd, died in 1789, after which his widow and two unmarried daughters let Mr Austen's parsonage at Deane. In 1792, the women were forced to vacate in favour of James Austen and his first wife, Anne Mathew. In 1797, after Anne died and James married Mary, she returned to the parsonage as mistress.

The Portal sisters were inspired by the heart-wrenching memorial to Mary Agnes, Cecilia and Augusta Knight (Jane Austen's great-nieces) at St Nicholas's church, Steventon. The three girls died in 1848, aged five, four and three years respectively, from scarlet fever, within days of each other.

The body in the cellar was inspired by an unknown woman whose partially mummified remains were discovered in a cellar in Bolton, England, in 1982. Her identity remains a mystery, despite being the subject of groundbreaking efforts to reconstruct a likeness of her face, but detectives working on the case nicknamed her 'Mary Ellen'.

Dr Jenner published *An Inquiry into the causes and effects of the variolæ vaccinæ* privately in 1798, after it was rejected by the Royal Society and for which he was initially much ridiculed. Austen records a party reading 'Dr Jenner's pamphlet on the cowpox' at Ashe Park in November 1800, and her friend, Anne Lefroy, vaccinated hundreds of her Hampshire neighbours. Dr Jenner's *Inquiry,* and efforts to promote mass vaccination, led directly to the eradication of smallpox.

Acknowledgements

In bringing this very special seasonal instalment of the *Miss Austen Investigates* series to the page, I am most grateful to:

My wonderful agent, Juliet Mushens, and everyone at Mushens Entertainment.

My incredible team at Penguin Michael Joseph, especially Maxine Hitchcock and Grace Long for giving me this opportunity, Phillipa Walker and Nick Lowndes (editorial), Hazel Orme (copy-editor), Sarah Davies (proofreader), Lily Evans (publicity), Jessica Parker (marketing), Nina Elstad (design), Helen Eka (production) and Kelly Mason (sales).

The hugely talented co-agents, publishers and translators who have made *Miss Austen Investigates* available to readers across the world.

The Austen biographers, scholars and historians whose work has proved invaluable to me, including: Deirdre Le Faye, Claire Tomalin, Rory Muir, Maria Hubert and Sarah Clegg.

All those who helped me discover specific facts about Austen and Christmas in the Eighteenth Century, especially: Jenny Colquhoun, St Nicholas Church (Steventon), The Vyne (National Trust) and Dyrham Park (National Trust).

The BBC podcast *The Forgotten Dead*, for introducing me to the case of the real 'Mary Ellen' and exploring the stories of missing and unidentified women.

My husband, Stephen, our daughters, Eliza and Rosina, and my dog Toby.

Finally, my readers – wishing you all a very merry celebration of Jane Austen's 250th birthday!